crimes
<small>of</small> passion

Gerard de Souza is a journalist based in Goa, with 15 years of experience in reporting on a wide range of issues, including politics, environment and crime. He also keenly follows criminal trials. His reporting on the death of a British teenager, Scarlett Keeling, and the subsequent trial of the alleged drug dealer and shack bartender—accused of conspiring to murder her—has earned him accolades. When not writing and reporting, he is busy fishing for clams, hunting for the best cashew *feni* or tending to his mango orchard.

crimes of passion

WHEN DESIRE TURNS DEADLY

GERARD de SOUZA

RUPA

Published by
Rupa Publications India Pvt. Ltd 2023
7/16, Ansari Road, Daryaganj
New Delhi 110002

Sales centres:
Bengaluru Chennai
Hyderabad Jaipur Kathmandu
Kolkata Mumbai Prayagraj

P-ISBN: 978-93-5702-520-1
E-ISBN: 978-93-5702-521-8

First impression 2023

10 9 8 7 6 5 4 3 2 1

The moral right of the author has been asserted.

Printed in India

To journalists from small towns and cities,
the silent storytellers of everyday India

CONTENTS

PROLOGUE
In the Name of Love

The saying, 'There's no such thing as a perfect crime' is oft-repeated by police investigators. It implies that no matter the circumstances, the culprit can always be caught.

But there definitely is something called a 'classic' crime—in the context of the stories listed herein—or at least a classic 'crime of passion'.

A crime of passion is a violent crime, especially homicide, in which the perpetrator commits the act against someone because of a sudden strong impulse. It can be from a sudden rage rather than a premeditated motive. But a 'classic' crime of passion involves a spouse who, upon finding their partner in bed with another, kills the romantic interloper in the heat of the moment.

That's exactly what Indian Navy officer Emile Jerome Mathew did. When he burst into his girlfriend's flat in Mumbai, having flown down all the way from the Kochi Naval base, he saw her in a compromising position with Neeraj Grover.

But not all crimes follow the same script. From jilted lovers murdering their exes to threatening harm to their family members, there's one common theme that runs through all the murders—love and rejection.

Women in Indian society are not expected to make decisions for themselves. They are expected to do the bidding of the men in their lives or else be prepared to face the consequences. In the stories in this book, these 'consequences' have inevitably meant death. Men aren't spared either. As several stories show, going up against caste and societal norms, and the wishes of someone more powerful, is a fatal choice.

There's a common 'mistake' all the victims in these stories have made. They dared to dream a life for themselves that didn't exactly follow the orders of those who thought otherwise. In India, that often means death.

1

DEATH BY A THOUSAND CUTS

The gruesome murder and dismemberment
of TV executive Neeraj Grover[1]

At 7.30 a.m. on 7 May 2008, Maria Monica Susairaj heard her doorbell ring. Still groggy from having slept late the previous night, Maria stumbled to the door. She had finally got possession of her sparsely furnished flat at 201, Dheeraj Solitaire—a plush residential high rise in the suburbs of Malad in Mumbai—only a day before. Having arrived in Mumbai a few days prior, she wasn't expecting any visitors.

Little did she know that what she was unlocking was not just the door of her newly acquired abode but a sequence of events that would change her life forever.

At 27 and yet to shed the prefix 'aspiring', the model and actress who grew up nurturing dreams of making it big in tinsel town was getting increasingly desperate. It

---

[1]Case details and quotations based on: State of Maharashtra v. Maria Monica Susairaj, Emile Jerome Joseph, Sessions Case No. 630 of 2008, Before the Court of Sessions for Gr Mumbai, 2011.

was her third stint in Mumbai, each of them justified as just 'one last shot' at stardom to revive a career that had stalled. With just three films to her credit—all back in her native state of Karnataka—and fearing that life was flying past her, Maria must have felt that it was now or never.

Maria Susairaj was the daughter of a real estate tycoon, among the most prominent in Mysore. From the age of five, she had taken to dance and was soon the toast of her school. This passion grew, and between 2002 and 2004, she acted in three Kannada films—*Joot* (2002), *Excuse Me* (2003) and *Ok Saar Ok* (2004). All of these were duds, in part owing to her ordinary acting skills. Where she did excel though was in the song and dance sequences. Not satisfied with her own performances, she enrolled at a dance studio in her hometown to improve her skill. She went on to briefly date the dance instructor, who later helped her find a toehold in Mumbai. At that time, the neatly organized streets of Mysore, the overarching trees and the closely knit Christian community created a web that enmeshed her spirit. Armed with a confident spirit, she made her way to Mumbai for the first time in 2005. After a three-month acting course spanning several classes, she tried to get the break she craved.

Mumbai and its rush have their own charm—a charm that can drown you out, or offer the freedom that many coming from small towns crave. It offers freedom from prying eyes of a small town, where everyone knows everyone and the world feels small. Life in the big city without the support of family is difficult for anyone. Landing the right contacts is often a deciding factor in a city full of glorified touts, schemers and self-styled agents.

For Maria, her entry into this world came through a boy named Neeraj. Hailing from Kanpur in Uttar Pradesh, the 25-year-old was relatively new to the city as well. The son of doting parents, Amarnath and Neelam Grover, left the dreary existence and roadside *dhabas* of the Hindi heartland and chose to embrace the glittering lights and Café-Coffee-Days of Mumbai. Living up to the reputation of being a casanova, Neeraj would unabashedly size up the nimble nymphs who gushed about his area of work with a twinkle in his eye. This twinkle would rarely go unrequited. You could count his relationships on the beads of a rosary.

Having worked with Balaji Telefilms Limited and rising quickly up the professional ladder as a creative producer, he was not short of offers. He soon found himself at Synergy Adlabs Media Ltd, another production house. This was in 2008, when the Mumbai entertainment industry was at its peak. It was a city whose media and entertainment industry was awash with cash and offers—a city blissfully unaware of the looming economic meltdown that was to hit mere months later.

∞

Maria and Neeraj met for the first time in 2007 during Maria's second stint in Mumbai. It wasn't exactly love at first sight. Their paths crossed at the many auditions that Maria was breezing through, hoping for a big break.

In March 2008, Maria reconnected with Neeraj and talked about her intentions to keep trying her luck in Mumbai. This was despite the odds, repeated rejections and her apparent predisposition to failure. Unlike many other small-town girls whose dreams slowly dissipate as they hope for the 'one break' that never comes, Maria could afford to keep trying. She always had the family business to fall back on if this didn't work out.

Neeraj got Maria an audition for the role of Draupadi in Balaji Telefilms' *Mahabharata* in March 2008. When it was apparent that it was not going to work out, she returned to Mysore. Neeraj lured Maria back to Mumbai, repeatedly promising that opportunities would be plenty and that something or the other would work out soon. He also made no bones about the fact that he wanted her in Mumbai not just to fulfil her dreams. He was in love with her. Torn between her dreams which seemed tantalizingly close and her plans of settling down in Mysore, Maria chose to cling to both.

She landed in Mumbai for her third stint on 29 April 2008 and caught up with Neeraj the same day. They picked up right where they had left off, this time without any inhibitions. Neeraj's close friend Nishant Lal later told the police that between 29 April 2008 and 6 May 2008, Neeraj and Maria met each other every day. He also mentioned how one evening he saw them kissing, while dancing at the D'Ultimate Pub.

However, it was not all mushy between the couple. Maria, Neeraj's friends later recalled, was keen on securing a role that Neeraj had promised to get her. However, they also said that she was beginning to doubt whether he was the right man for the job. Their relationship was a curious one. While Neeraj was prepared to go any lengths to please his newly found 'mate', Maria was clearly on a mission and he merely represented a stepping stone for her. Being lured to Mumbai only to realize that Neeraj wasn't all that he promised was something that was playing havoc with Maria's mind.

On 6 May 2008, Maria got her new flat. That evening, Neeraj didn't hang out with his friends at their usual coffee shop. Instead, he went to see Maria. When his friends called him to join them, he said that Maria needed his help with shifting. Later, when his roommates called him to attend a festive dinner at their shared flat, he declined and gave the same excuse. That was the last time his friends heard from him.

Later, Maria's testimony at the court offered a different narration of the events that transpired. She said:

> [...] At about 11 pm when I came out from [the] house of my neighbour after taking a bath there, I saw that Neeraj was at the door of my house. I had introduced him to my neighbour... We then entered my house. I asked him as to why he came... He said that he wanted to give help to arrange my house... Though Neeraj was called by his friends to attend the party, he did not go. I had also refused to join him at the party. Neeraj had work in the morning at Malad. So, he had requested me to allow him to stay... I said that it is OK and he stayed...

Perhaps, it was only unpacking that was taking place right up to four that morning. That is when the duo reportedly dozed off exhausted in each other's arms.

One can imagine an eerie calm settling on the flat, broken only by the ebb and flow of the nearby Malad creek. This was until the urgent buzzing of the doorbell pierced through the calmness at 7.30 a.m. on 7 May 2008.

∞

On the other side of the door stood Lieutenant Emile Jerome Mathew. As a young and bright officer, Emile was on the brink of a long and illustrious career with the navy. He and Maria hailed from the same hometown, but came from different worlds. Emile was well-built and surefooted. He excelled not just in academics but also in athletics, and stood out for his good looks and confident nature.

Soon after his twelfth standard, Emile attempted to get into one of the many IITs (Indian Institute of Technology) in the country. When he failed, he settled for the four-year naval engineers' course at INS Shivaji in Lonavala in 2000. He was well respected among his mates, not just because of his tough physique but also for his mild manners and commitment to his work. He was, after all, a stickler for getting a job done well. While he dreamt of being a marine commando, his bosses did not allow it, as he had been trained as an engineer.

No one can fully explain what made Emile and Maria stick together. They had met in 2007 via the now-defunct social networking site Orkut that was all the rage back then. It is often suggested that it was Maria's sister, Veronica, who nudged them to get together. Perhaps her suggestion was only in jest, and not born out of some gut feeling that the duo would make a good pair. They were soon a serious couple, and even agreed to settle down.

It is possible that Emile saw in Maria the possibility of a trophy wife—one he could show off to his friends, a trophy that he had plucked out right from the movie screen. Or maybe there was something in her that really pulled him in. With Emile choosing to keep his counsel throughout the trial and subsequent incarceration, we will never know.

Maria, on the other hand, had previously had a string of relationships. During the trial, she herself admitted that she didn't take any of her previous relationships seriously. She perhaps saw in Emile a man who was 'marriage material'— stable, committed and clearly in love with her.

Maria's parents had no qualms about her marriage with Emile. But Emile had battled with his family to try and convince them that she was the ideal woman for him. It was not surprising that a deeply traditional Catholic family from Kerala's Wayanad looked disapprovingly on a 'loose-looking' girl from the showbiz industry. Her gyrating on-screen moves probably made them squirm in discomfort. That she also hailed from a Catholic family provided little relief. Neither Emile nor his family softened their respective stands about Maria.

Emile and Maria chatted regularly, even if they couldn't meet as much. He was posted at the INS Garuda Naval Base in Kochi, and she constantly kept moving from Mumbai to Bangalore or Mysore (and vice versa). Nonetheless, plans for their wedding were well underway. Maria is said to have referred to Emile as her fiancé, when introducing him to her old friends. Emile too made it clear among his mates that he was serious about Maria.

ॐ

However, all was not well. Maria was two-timing Emile. She had hidden the nature of her relationship with Neeraj from Emile, only mentioning that he was helping her scout for roles. The two men had never met. In her confession before a magistrate, she made it sound like it was Neeraj who was the eager one in the relationship. But there was no evidence suggesting that she was only a reluctant participant, playing along for the purpose of securing a role.

Emile was in regular touch with Maria, and had spoken to her several times on 6 May 2008, the last being at 11.30 p.m. For much of the time that Neeraj was at her flat, Maria was on the phone with Emile. On the call, Emile heard a male voice laughing in the background. Neeraj may have acted cocky and indignant. Emile reportedly proceeded to enquire who was in her flat at such a late hour. Maria told him it was Neeraj, who was helping her move in. She told Emile that he would not be staying over, specifically mentioning that she would ask him to leave. They spoke for nearly an hour. Since her phone battery was low, she asked Emile to call on Neeraj's phone. She then gave Neeraj's number to Emile.

'What kind of boyfriend is he that he needs another man to be with her?' Neeraj reportedly said while handing over his phone to Maria. That statement probably snapped something within Emile, and that changed his life forever.

At the base, one of his mates found Emile pacing up-and-down and visibly disturbed. Upon enquiry, instead of telling his friend the truth, Emile said that his fiancée needed his help and that he needed to be with her immediately. A ticket on board a 3.45 a.m. Air India flight to Mumbai was booked and Emile asked to borrow a friend's motorcycle to get to the airport.

His friend, seeing that he was trembling, offered to drop him off. He feared that Emile was in no condition to ride the bike and would end up hurting himself. It was only later that his friend realized that it was not fear but rage that made Emile tremble. Emile left without applying for a leave of absence from his commanding officer, and was standing outside Maria's door at 7.30 a.m.

There were no independent eyewitnesses for what transpired next, and all we have is Maria's confessional statement from the court document. This statement was very obviously offered with an aim of trying to absolve herself of any guilt.

Emile marched in to find his fiancée in a flimsy nightdress. Neeraj, who had only just woken up, was lying naked on her bed. 'He directly entered my house. I followed Emile as he marched straight to the bedroom,' Maria recounted. Based on her statement, Neeraj then cockily proceeded to say, 'Is this your boyfriend?'

Neeraj mistakenly thought that it was the right time for him to resume his cockiness from the previous night. But Emile was furious. 'Immediately, thereafter, Emile started giving fist blows to Neeraj. Both started fighting with each other. I could not control them,' Maria recalled before the judge. She said that she tried to break up the fight only to be thrown away. She injured herself in the process, and was left with 'deep gashes' on her palms.[2] A medical examination later revealed that these gashes were caused by a knife—the knife wielded by Emile.

Neeraj (a creative producer) was no match for Emile (a trained combatant, considered tough even by Navy standards), and was soon overpowered. Emile then rushed to grab a

---

[2]'You, Madame, are My Suspect Number One', *Mumbai Mirror*, 1 July 2011, http://bit.ly/3X8Z4vD. Accessed on 7 June 2023.

knife. As Mumbai Police Commissioner Rakesh Maria later recalled, Emile then stabbed Neeraj several times in the chest and abdomen.[3] He could hardly have been exaggerating. By the time Maria, who had been thrown to the floor in the melee, got up, she saw that Neeraj was already stabbed.

'Maria! Maria!' Neeraj reportedly called as he fell to the floor. But it was all over in a matter of minutes.

Special Judge M.W. Chandwani, in his order convicting Emile of culpable homicide with the intent, said: 'To find a young man with his young fiancée, that too during odd hours, obviously, for a fiancé is a provoking situation, to lose his self-control. So, a prudent man will lose his self-control... was impelled to lose his control to find a young man with his fiancée's home during [an] odd hour.'

As Neeraj's dead body lay next to them, Emile and Maria made love—a love that was laden with emotions in each thrust. Then they did it again—this time in the bathroom. In her confession, Maria said that she was raped. All this happened while Neeraj lay in a pool of blood that slowly darkened from red to deep maroon. The blood on the mattress and the wall had already dried up.

But the horrors were only just beginning...

Neeraj was scheduled to meet television actress Barsha Chatterjee at seven that morning. She noticed that Neeraj had failed to meet their appointment. At that time, she didn't think it was anything serious.

[3]Panigrahi, Debasish, "'It Took me Four Hours to Chop Body'", *Hindustan Times*, 24 May 2008, https://bit.ly/3MT7aUf. Accessed on 7 June 2023.

The first to panic was Neeraj's mother, Neelam. Every morning and evening Neelam would call her son unfailingly, as mothers are wont to do. When the first call at around 10.00 a.m. remained unanswered, she thought that maybe he had overslept. Maybe he had kept his phone aside to take a shower or was preoccupied with something else. But then half an hour later, the next call too went unanswered and then the next and the next... What was a mild concern soon became a worry—a major worry turning into full-blown panic.

At around noon, Maria called Nishant (Neeraj's close friend, with whom she was acquainted) to tell him that Neeraj left her home the previous night at 1.30 a.m. but had left his phone behind. She asked him to come and collect it. By 1.00 p.m., Maria called a friend, asking whether she could borrow his Santro car. She promised to return it before 9.30 p.m.

Maria visited the Hypercity Mall in Malad and bought rexine sports bags, a fresh set of drapes, room freshener and a bread knife. She later told the police that she was acting under duress, after being threatened by Emile with dire consequences. However, she betrayed none of that duress as she calmly went about shopping.

The body was chopped to 'pieces', Police Commissioner Rakesh Maria said while addressing a press conference on 21 May 2008. This was two weeks after the murder took place, and the case had finally been cracked.[4]

It took Emile four hours to butcher Neeraj's body, which he said was slow because the knife quickly lost its edge.

---

[4]Ibid.

Emile sawed through the tough tissue in the bathroom, while keeping the tap running to ensure the blood was quickly washed off. Maria helped him put the pieces in the bags that she had purchased from the mall.

News channels later reported that Neeraj's body was chopped into 300 pieces, a figure that even shocked the trial judge. He questioned how the reporters carved the figure out of thin air. The reality was that it was around 6–8 pieces. Emile had carefully sawed off the joints to fit them into the suitcases.

Emile loaded the body parts into the bags. Maria proceeded to clean the house, changed the drapes and dumped the kitchen knife in a bathroom drain pipe, hoping it would never be found. They even called a painter who assured them of a visit the next day.

At around 4.30 p.m., the duo loaded the bags into the borrowed car while the building's security guard curiously looked on. They lugged the heavy bags, each holding one end, and loaded them in the car before driving off towards Manorwada (far outside the city). They bought a jerry can of petrol at Bhayandar, and a lighter along the way. They set Neeraj's remains alight whilst making sure that there was no one who noticed them. When Maria later took the police to the spot, all that remained was pieces of his rib cage and skull; bits of burnt cloth; beads and a metal button; and a chain and arm band. The police relied on these remains for further investigation.

By 9.30 p.m., Maria and Emile were back at the Malad flat. They were confident that they had successfully pulled off the most outrageous cover-up. In reality, they did leave behind a trail of crumbs for Rakesh Maria and the Crime

Branch to follow. Maria carried Neeraj's mobile phone wherever she went. This proved to be a fatal mistake.

∽

By that time, Neeraj's family and friends were panicking. From around 10.00 a.m. until 9.30 p.m., there were around 130 missed calls on Neeraj's phone. All except one went unanswered. This was a call from Neeraj's sister Shika's phone. She was desperately trying to get in touch all day. But all she heard was a breezy bustling and some distant voices before the call got disconnected. The call was accidentally received as the phone lay in Maria's pocket while she was picking up the Santro Car. It was the phone that finally helped the police unravel the case, and call Maria and Emile's bluff. Until then, Maria played her part to the T.

Neeraj's friends Nishant Lal and cousin Nishant Grover arrived at Maria's flat to collect his mobile phone. Rather than welcoming them to the flat, Maria chose to meet them downstairs. She handed Neeraj's phone to Nishant, and accompanied him to the Malad police station to lodge a missing complaint. She even cried when asked about his whereabouts.

After returning from there, Maria and Emile spent some time together carefully discussing what they would tell the police. They needed to ensure that their stories matched, and didn't arouse suspicion. The next morning, she and Emile gave their statements to the police feigning ignorance of Neeraj's whereabouts. They were pretty confident that their cover-up had worked. The couple even had lunch outside, and Emile returned to the naval base on 9 May 2008.

Meanwhile, Neeraj's family began frantically looking for him. His father Amarnath flew down from Kanpur and began scouting unclaimed bodies. He looked alongside railway tracks and scanned random faces in the street in a bid to find his son. He was soon putting up posters with the help of friends and family, hoping people would come forward and offer clues about his son. With the police making no headway, Amarnath approached the Crime Branch of the Mumbai Police. The Crime Branch then began a parallel investigation.

When initially questioned by the police, Maria claimed she was shopping in Dadar the afternoon after the murder. When it was presented to her that a call had been received on Neeraj's phone in Andheri and not Dadar, she began to break down. The location of Neeraj's mobile at around 7.30 p.m. was shown to be on the way to Manorwada, something Maria was unable to explain to the police.

Two weeks was all it took for the Crime Branch to have her singing like a canary. The police built a case that this was a pre-planned conspiracy by Maria and Emile to eliminate Neeraj. They showed the motive to be Maria feeling used, since Neeraj had failed to secure her the promised role. The most incriminating bit of evidence to support the 'conspiracy' theory was that Emile had actually booked his flight to Mumbai at 9.00 p.m. that night, much before Neeraj had come to Maria's flat. As mentioned earlier, it was only at around 11.00 p.m. that Neeraj had ended up at her doorstep.

Did Maria call Neeraj over despite knowing that Emile would be arriving the following morning? It was a theory that the judge didn't buy. The judge stressed that everything about Emile's departure, the murder and subsequent cover-up seemed to be spur-of-the-moment decisions rather than a well-planned conspiracy.

Throughout the trial, Emile maintained a stoic expression. He only winced sometimes, if the lawyers made arguments that did not reflect the sequence of events as he had witnessed them. The trial judge too noted that 'whenever, there was any irregularity on behalf of the prosecution, [Jerome] promptly objected'.

Maria's confession retraced the entire sequence. She withdrew her confession later, claiming that it was extracted under pressure. She pleaded innocence and even offered an alibi.

༄

On 1 July 2011, a little more than three years after the murder—after the testimonies and cross examination of 48 witnesses—Accused No. 1 Maria Monica Susairaj was sentenced to three years imprisonment for her role in destroying the evidence. She was acquitted of murder and conspiracy to kill Neeraj. This verdict left Neeraj's friends and family aghast, considering the gruesomeness of the cover-up.

It was her confession, even though it wasn't accepted as evidence by the sessions court, that helped save her. Maria successfully convinced the court that she had no role in the murder—only in the cover-up. This was despite the prosecution arguing that both Emile and Maria murdered Neeraj. In the absence of eyewitnesses, and with Emile choosing to not take his fiancée down with him, Maria was freed soon after the verdict. She had already served the duration of her sentence.

Accused No. 2 Emile was convicted of culpable homicide with the intent to kill, and sentenced to 10 years' rigorous imprisonment and three years for destroying evidence. His appeal is still pending before the Bombay High Court, but he completed the duration of his sentence in 2018.

Maria's life changed forever after this. As of 2019, she was a career criminal along with one Paromita Chakraborty (whom she befriended in jail while under trial). The police said Susairaj and Chakraborty became friends when they were lodged in Byculla prison between 2010 and 2012.[5]

In 2015, Maria was arrested by the Vadodara Police for her alleged involvement in the ₹2.11 crore Haj air ticket scam along with Paromita. In 2018, Maria was arrested again for duping a businessman of ₹2.72 crore.[6] The duo, along with others, had promised to help the businessman obtain a bank loan at low-interest rates. There are seven complaints, mainly deregistered, against Maria and her partners-in-crime Paromita Chakraborty and Anita Vedpathak.

Emile headed home after the period of his sentence elapsed. Perhaps, he finally put his engineering skills to good use.

Journalist Meenal Bhagel put together an acclaimed book, *Death in Mumbai*, on the killing. In an interview a few months after the convictions, she said: 'Look at the way it all—the killing—became Maria's fault. She became the big

---

[5]'Maria Susairaj Named in 7 Complaints of Cheating with Her Partner', *Mumbai Mirror*, 26 March 2019, https://bit.ly/42xhLv6. Accessed on 23 March 2023.
[6]Raja, Aditi, 'Vadodara Court Remands Maria Susairaj to 4-Day Police Custody', *The Indian Express*, 10 October 2015, https://tinyurl.com/4534zytc. Accessed on 27 July 2023.

villainess, whereas during my research I found, in certain quarters, a grudging respect for Emile's actions as he had, after all, found his fiancée with another man.'[7]

At a time when she was hoping that some doors of opportunity would open for her, Maria opened the door to her downfall. She will probably spend the rest of her life wishing she had done things differently. While the story may gradually fade away from memory, the scars will remain.

[7]Bhattacharya, Sanchari, "'Maria Susairaj was Confused, Vulnerable, Manipulative and Stupid'", *Rediff.com*, 2 December 2011, https://bit.ly/3Z6i9O9. Accessed on 23 March 2023.

2

SHOOTING FOR THE MOON

*The murder of the mother and uncle
of danseuse Moon Das*

It was past midnight when the otherwise buzzing Oshiwara Police Station began to wind down. Constables, who would usually be dealing with complainants or rustling through paperwork, began to feel the first yawns creeping up on them and tried to fight it off with gossip. In the midst of a very mundane Thursday night, a woman and her guy friend burst through the gates of the *thana* and went right to the receiving desk.

The Oshiwara Police Station keeps an eye on the several well-known, and sometimes controversial, TV production houses that occupy large blocks within the station's jurisdiction. These production houses oversee soap operas worth crores of rupees, and have even come to define the locality. Celebrities, creatives and backstage staff mix and mingle there.

Moon Das and Romesh Sharma burst into the police station. They had been running as fast as they could for half a kilometre or so, from her residence in New Link Garden

(Yamuna Nagar, Andheri) straight to the police station—like it was a matter of life or death. And it was!

∽

Moushumi Das, popularly known as Moon, had moved from North Kolkata to Mumbai in search of a fast-paced and freedom-filled life. Little did she know that it would be the fast pace of her feet, thudding on the uneven tarmac of suburban Mumbai, on 22 November 2007 that would come to define her. Daughter of a furniture shop owner in Bowbazar, Moon used to look on in awe as Aishwarya Rai and Sushmita Sen dazzled the world by winning the Miss World and Miss Universe beauty pageants respectively. The lure of the pageant may have since faded, but back then two brown-skinned girls making it to the top of a global contest was something that had the nation's attention. In a country where the most a woman could aspire to—if they weren't exceptionally bright—was being a wife, their win became an anomaly.

As days turned to weeks, months and years, Moon's father realized that her obsession with pageantry was not just a phase. He made his dislike for the same very well-known. But her desire to take a plunge into modelling, her persistent spirit, her blackmailing tactics and unstinting support from her mother, saw Moon on the covers of several fashion magazines. She was soon a regular at shows where models were in demand.

When she was 17, Bollywood superstar Shah Rukh Khan (SRK) visited Kolkata for an event. She made a connection with one of the organizers, who ensured that she was among the many models on stage when the King of Bollywood made his appearance. She even managed to get paid for it. Her skills to manage such feats went on to serve her well in life.[1]

She made friends with the other models at the SRK show, and through them began to scout for more modelling opportunities. She was soon modelling for a Bengali women's magazine, *Sananda,* and also for designers Mona Lamba and Pali Sachdev.

Her first beauty pageant was the Gladrags Manhunt and Megamodel Contest, in which she was selected and called to Mumbai for the finals. In the 20 days she spent in Mumbai, she fell in love with the city. She later told author Meenal Bhagel in an interview (detailed in the book *Death in Mumbai*) that she realized Mumbai gave her the freedom that Kolkata did not. She said: 'It was fantastic. I could go anywhere, at any time, do what I liked. I realised that in this city everything depends on you. Nothing else matters and that was such a heady discovery.'[2] She started staying on her own in Mumbai, in a rented accommodation.

She didn't win the contest, but she got a valuable toehold in an industry where contacts and acquaintances are everything. She began calling fellow models she had met at the Gladrags contest. But it was like running into a wall repeatedly. Finally, she did manage to be invited to a 'Page 3' party, which helped her get noticed in no small measure. She wore an outfit that made heads turn. It helped

---

[1]Baghel, Meenal, *Death in Mumbai: A True Story*, Random House India, 1 December 2011.
[2]Ibid.

her model for print ads, and other odd modelling jobs but didn't really take her very far.

She discovered that there indeed was a glass ceiling that prevented her from bursting into the world of film which, for many models, is the next logical step. Perhaps, it was her dusky skin tone—still a deal-breaker for many—or the fact that she wasn't really mingling in the right circles. She was forced into doing live shows as an 'item girl'—a crass term for a voluptuous dancer at industry parties. This soon became her mainstay.

These were the high growth years for the Indian economy. Corporate parties were aplenty, and song and dance were the preferred form of entertainment. The stand-up comics were still about a decade away from becoming mainstream.

Maybe it was her luscious moves or her approachable demeanour, but Moon was soon the hot property at these parties. As her popularity grew, so did the competition. Finding work became difficult in an increasingly crowded market. Moon found herself accepting shows away from corporate parties. These shows took her to family functions and weddings in areas that were away from metropolitan cities. She soon realized how different life away from the cities can be.

∽

It was at a show in Rourkela (eastern Odisha) on New Year's Eve in 2006 that Moon was introduced to Avinash Patnaik. He was the son of a superintending engineer of Western Electric Supply Company in Sambalpur. He was 22, a year younger than Moon. After the end of the show, when she retired to her room, the organizer knocked on her door with Avinash in tow. He offered to show her around town. Whether she mistook the offer as a sincere gesture by well-meaning folk, or whether she saw through the ruse of a man wanting to be privately introduced to her...we don't know.

The next day, she was taken around town. She described that as a charming tour, which included tea at a college canteen. She politely promised to return the favour, should either of the two (the organizer or Avinash) choose to visit Mumbai.[3]

Avinash took this offer seriously. He abruptly showed up in Mumbai and Moon, true to her word, showed him around the big city. In an interview with *The Times of India*, Moon later recalled: 'He was this small-town guy who was curious and excited about life in a big city like Mumbai. When he came down to Mumbai, I took him out shopping at Lokhandwala, got him the latest hairstyles and groomed him in general.'[4]

They were soon in a relationship. Moon's eagerness to not enter relationships with people within the industry owing to their 'fly-by-night' nature; the lure of financial stability brought by Avinash; and the fact that love can be blind, all played their part in bringing the two together. On the surface, Avinash was a 'nice boy'—that's how his family later described him[5]—along with being sensitive and

---

[3]Ibid.

[4]Natu, Nitasha, 'He Needed Help, I had Told his Family: Moon', *The Times of India*, 26 November 2007, https://bit.ly/40kOEt4. Accessed on 23 March 2023.

[5]Sahu, Priya Ranjan, 'Killer was a "Nice Boy"', *Hindustan Times*, 25 November 2007, https://bit.ly/3LIUkZE. Accessed on 23 March 2023.

helpful. He also had an enterprising streak. He had, with the help of a ₹2-crore bank loan, started a rice mill in Jarapada (Odisha) in 2005.

Moon later recalled, 'What attracted me to Avinash initially was his loving and caring nature.'[6] He is said to have deposited ₹5 lakh in her bank account, to help her make a music video. She accepted this despite her doubts, and against her better judgement. It was a transaction that later came back to haunt her.

A few months into the relationship, the gloss faded. It turned out Avinash was extremely possessive, to the point of being toxic. It was a long-distance relationship, and he wanted to know all the minute details of Moon's life—who she was meeting, when, where and to what end. At one point, Moon even volunteered to give up her career. Avinash thought that the demands of the industry and the seductive acts she needed to perform were more than the relationship could take.

When he was with her, Avinash would insist that she dress up and behave boldly. Perhaps, he did this to help her prop up his self-esteem. Maybe he wanted to be the object of envy among friends and onlookers. But Moon, who knew the boundaries between what she did on-stage and in real life, was very uncomfortable.

Things reached a head when one evening back in Rourkela, Avinash offered to take Moon to a disco and asked her to dress flashier than usual. It was later that night

---

[6]Natu, Nitasha, 'He Needed Help, I had Told his Family: Moon', *The Times of India*, 26 November 2007, https://bit.ly/40kOEt4. Accessed on 23 March 2023.

that Moon realized, much to her horror, that Avinash was at the disco to ask the owner for a loan and had offered Moon as the collateral!

She flatly refused. This sparked a bitter fight—their worst yet—and it ended with Avinash consuming sleeping pills. Moon was unfazed by this. She herself had tried the trick of taking an overdose of sleeping pills—just enough to knock her out, but not kill her—in an effort to convince her father to give a go-ahead for her modelling career. She waited for Avinash to wake up before resuming the argument.[7]

The next morning, Avinash woke up remorseful and seemed to regret the events of the previous night. They visited a temple and asked a priest to bless their union. Later, Moon did not accept this marriage. 'I was not married to him. *Mandir mein tika lagane se shaadi nahin ho jaati* [Just putting a mark on the forehead in a temple doesn't mean a marriage has taken place],' she later said in an interview.[8]

Avinash asked Moon to return to Mumbai, promising to call her back as soon as his financial situation improved. But the truce proved short-lived. A mere four days later, Avinash showed up at Moon's apartment in Mumbai. She was now living with her mother's brother, Vikas Sarkar. Being completely in the dark about the goings-on in her personal life, Vikas was left confused by the unknown man showing up at his door with the intention of staying over.

---

[7]Baghel, Meenal, *Death in Mumbai: A True Story*, Random House India, 1 December 2011.

[8]Lalwani, Vickey, 'After Eviction, Moon Das in Trouble', *The Times of India*, 1 March 2009, https://bit.ly/3FLcqX9. Accessed on 23 March 2023.

Vikas saw how bad things were. Every time Moon and Avinash would argue, Avinash would strike out at Moon. He did this even in front of her friends. She would sometimes end up bruised, bleeding or with something broken. Flimsy reasons would lead to fights—her dressing sense, whom she was meeting, the fact that she had photoshoots lined up.[9] His possessive nature only worsened with two vicious habits he developed in Mumbai—alcohol and drugs. This was not uncommon among debt-ridden and unemployed youth, both in big cities and small towns.

The relationship deteriorated quickly. Later in an interview, Moon said: 'My uncle saw the injuries on my body once and told Avinash that [even] my own family had never hit me.'[10] She claimed that she had mentioned Avinash's abusive behaviour to his brother Pritam. While sounding sympathetic, Pritam would tell her that only she could bring a change in Avinash.

As the abuse continued, her uncle summoned her mother (Kanan Das) to Mumbai. The two seniors ensured that Avinash packed his bags and returned to Odisha.

༄

By 2 October 2007, just about 10 months after they had met each other, Moon decided enough was enough and cut off ties with Avinash. She stopped engaging with him and tried her best to avoid him. She chose to bury herself in

---

[9]Natu, Nitasha, 'He Needed Help, I had Told his Family: Moon', *The Times of India*, 26 November 2007, https://bit.ly/40kOEt4. Accessed on 23 March 2023.
[10]Ibid.

her work, travelled abroad for shows and kept herself busy.

She would intermittently receive his calls in which he would threaten, blackmail and try every trick in the book to get the relationship back on track. A private detective in Mumbai even confirmed that he received a call from Avinash, wherein he made inquiries about the rates and feasibility of keeping an eye on Moon.[11]

In Avinash's perverse and stubborn mind, the only reason Moon had dumped him was because she had found someone else. The more he thought about it, the more convinced he became that this was the only logical explanation. Moon later recalled, 'He had somehow started believing that I was seeing someone else, even when I wasn't.'[12]

Avinash came up with a plan, desperately trying to reach a conclusion. It involved a country revolver and three bullets. He planned to threaten to kill himself, to force her to get back with him. If she didn't relent, he planned to kill her and then himself. He had kept the third bullet just as a backup. Armed with the gun, he set off from Angul for Mumbai. This was on 21 November 2007.

It's a long drive from Angul to Mumbai. It is a journey that cuts across the heart of India and takes most people the best part of three days (with rest). However, with no breaks, Avinash completed the journey in a little over 24 hours. The long drive and open stretches of the Deccan

---

[11]'Cops Looking at Mystery Scrapper in Moon's Case', *Mumbai Mirror*, 27 November 2007, https://tinyurl.com/5xaauvsn. Accessed on 11 July 2023.
[12]Natu, Nitasha, 'He Needed Help, I had Told his Family: Moon', *The Times of India*, 26 November 2007, https://bit.ly/40kOEt4. Accessed on 23 March 2023.

Plateau did little to soothe his mind that was still smarting, unable to digest Moon's rejection.

∽

On 22 November 2007, Moon was going about her day as usual. At around 7.00 p.m., as she was on her way to a meeting with LG Electronics (in connection with an advertising campaign), she received a call from Avinash. She spoke for a while, and Avinash once again made his pitch imploring her to get back with him. It was a mix of blackmail, threats, begging and mostly anything to cling on to her.

Avinash calling her and trying to reconcile with her was now a run-of-the-mill occurrence. She had no clue that he was already in Mumbai with a revolver in his car's glove compartment. The call was, in fact, a last-ditch effort to get her to change her mind. Since she was in a meeting after that, Moon ignored her phone for the rest of the evening. She followed up her meeting with a dinner at Garden Court restaurant in Andheri.

It was during dinner, at around 11.00 p.m., that she decided to check on her mother (whom she had last spoken to at around 9.30 p.m.). She tried calling her mother and when she didn't pick up the phone, she called her uncle who didn't answer either.

She got a sick feeling in her gut and rushed home. She asked her friend Romesh Sharma to accompany her. They drove quickly to her residence, arriving a little past midnight. Her fears quickly turned to dread after she saw Avinash's Honda City parked in the apartment complex.

With each passing second, Moon's fear only kept getting worse. But she was completely unprepared for what came next. When she rang the doorbell, it was Avinash who opened the door, holding the revolver. The door was only partially open, and she could not see anyone else through the door. As she stood at the door, Avinash grabbed her arm and attempted to yank her inside the flat. With some help from her friend and as the door was not completely open, Moon freed herself from Avinash's grip and pulled the door shut. They bolted it from the outside. They ran for their lives through the mazy obstacle-ridden streets of suburban Mumbai, until they found themselves panting and breathless at the Oshiwara Police Station.

When the cops entered the flat, Avinash lay by the window, still warm and quivering as fresh blood rushed out of his temple. This was where the bullet had pierced through. There is a probability that he might have seen or heard the police entering the building. As the main door was locked, he had no chance of escaping.

The colder bodies of Kanan Das and Vikas Sarkar were found in the bedroom—a bullet each had punched a hole in their chests.

The events of the day will most probably haunt Moon forever. She was unable to forgive herself, for she knew that her mother and uncle had lost their lives instead of her. Did Avinash kill her mother and uncle immediately, or did he torture them before pulling the trigger? Did they die quickly or did they suffer? She was the primary target, and it was only her presence of mind to bolt the door from the outside that saved her. Moon was felicitated by the Lions' Club of Mumbai for her presence of mind, which they said had saved her life.

Shockingly, this was only the beginning—a beginning of a wholly different ordeal in which she was made the arch villain; a femme fatale par excellence. As is the case most of the time, the blame for the turn of events are thrown mostly at the woman. Why would Moon's case be any different?

Soon, both Moon's and Avinash's families rushed to Mumbai. Avinash's family quickly turned on Moon and accused her of murdering him. They accused her of being a gold-digger and of conspiring to have him eliminated. Avinash's father, Bhupen Patnaik, told the reporters, 'The bullet that killed Avinash was shot through his left temple whereas he was a right-hander.' He was making an argument that a right hander would have naturally placed the pistol to his right temple.[13]

The investigating officer, however, countered the query saying that the hole in the left temple was made by the bullet exiting his forehead. Hence, it was larger than the one on the right. But the family was not convinced. Bhupen insisted, 'A fashionable and jolly person cannot commit such a crime.'[14]

The murders and suicide left many unanswered questions. Why did Avinash travel all the way from Odisha to Mumbai with only three bullets? No spare bullets were found in the car. Was the gun only to be used as a means to threaten Moon? Had he not anticipated that Moon's family, at least

---

[13]'Conspiracy behind Mumbai Tripple Murder?', *Odisha.in*, 27 November 2007, https://bit.ly/3JB6KAh. Accessed on 23 March 2023.

[14]'Open and Shut Case: Cops', *DNA*, 19 November 2013, https://bit.ly/3K2bf8m. Accessed on 23 March 2023.

her uncle, would be in the flat with her? Why did he enter the flat without being sure that Moon, the most crucial ingredient of his plan, was at home? How could Avinash, an amateur, snuff out two adults at point-blank range with a bullet each?

In an interview with *The Indian Express*, Bhupen Patnaik talked of his doubts at length:

> We came to Mumbai, and heard a completely one-sided story from the police there. There was no way of verifying what had happened. We had never heard of Moon Das. We went to Bhubaneswar on the way back home (Angul), and recovered Avinash's personal laptop.[...] On checking the laptop, I saw that Avinash had transferred Rs 5 lakh to Moon Das's account on February 14 this year.[15]

He also said that Avinash had spent several lakhs to buy and apartment for Moon Das and her mother in Kolkata. The sum he had spent totalled about ₹60 lakh. Bhupen said that some close friends of Avinash told him that he gave ₹40 lakh to Romesh Sharma, so that he could help Moon get some roles in films.[16]

༒

For the police, this was an open-and-shut case. With the help of forensics, they quickly ruled out possibilities other

---

[15]Chowdhury, Sagnik, 'Father Claims Avinash Spent Lakhs to Kickstart Das's Career', *The Indian Express*, 26 November 2007, https://bit.ly/3n8mF1f. Accessed on 23 March 2023.
[16]Ibid.

than a murder–suicide. The case then faded away from media attention.

However, Moon continued to live with the consequences. She was now no longer the struggling performer eager to rise up the charts. In an interview with an entertainment tabloid, Moon said: 'People would see me and run away. I had practically locked myself in Pataliputra Apartments. [...] But after having lived there for 10 months, the society found out my identity and asked me to leave. I tried arguing with them and refused to leave immediately.'[17] In December 2008, she shifted to another apartment complex.

She later admitted that she had been with the wrong man. Avinash had constant arguments with her uncle and mother, and her father had also disliked him. She once said: 'I have put all that behind me. And I am not close to loving somebody again. I want to do some good work now. I have realised that you need a name and money to survive in this society.'[18]

Moon dawdled in a few celebrity-linked reality shows in the few years after this life-altering event but eventually faded from the spotlight. Her life came full circle when she was warmly welcomed home by her family, especially her father. Unlike before, he encouraged her to continue chasing her dream exactly how her mother would have wanted.

She was briefly back in the news in 2009 when she accused Flynn Remedios of stalking her, and sending her lewd messages. When she blocked him, he uploaded her number

---

[17]'A Das(h) of Courage', *Mumbai Mirror*, 27 February 2009, https://bit.ly/40aShSz. Accessed on 23 March 2023.
[18]Ibid.

on a pornography website.[19] Moon had to run from pillar to post to ensure her complaint was registered, and even then the police showed no interest in netting the culprit.

In 2014, Moon was back in the news after a minor road accident resulted in a skirmish with Sidharth Bharadwaj (an MTV VJ [video jockey]). She said that he threatened to tear her clothes if she did not pay ₹30,000 for the damage to his car.[20]

Speaking in a completely different context, author and journalist Meghna Pant said: 'If you're a woman in India— be scared. Our country would rather label you a murderer, social climber, gold digger, witch, drug dealer, man eater and liar, than admit that a man can suffer from mental health issues.'[21]

She could very well have been referring to the events surrounding the Moon Das case.

---

[19]'Web-Snared Moon Goes to Cops', *The Times of India*, 3 October 2008, https://tinyurl.com/w79e69ee. Accessed on 27 July 2023.

[20]Maheshwri, Neha, 'Sidharth Bharadwaj: Molestation Too Strong a Word to Be Used Casually', *ETimes*, 12 August 2014, https://tinyurl.com/3vydra3c. Accessed on 27 July 2023.

[21]@MeghnaPant, Twitter, 27 August 2020, 10.37 p.m., https://tinyurl.com/yc3bbuwv. Accessed on 23 June 2023.

3

SCARLETT-STAINED SANDS

*The rape and murder of British teenager Scarlett
Keeling, found dead on a Goa beach*[1]

A t around 5.30 a.m. on 18 February 2008, Fidelis D'Souza,
a retired cop from the Central Industrial Security Force,
was on his usual morning walk along the Anjuna beach
in Goa. Sunrise was a little more than an hour away. For
D'Souza, this was the best hour to be at the beach, as he
could have the entire space to himself. 5.30 a.m. is early
even by most joggers' standards. As a man of discipline,
D'Souza was briskly pacing along the shore.

In the faint light of daybreak, D'Souza spotted a girl
lying in the sand. As he neared, he noticed that she was
lying motionless with the waves lapping against her glazed
face. The girl was completely naked, with only her unhooked
brassiere lying loosely over her neck and shoulder. A
shocked D'Souza abruptly cut short his morning walk, and

---

[1]Quotes and case details from the document: Central Bureau of
Investigation v. Samson D'Souza, Criminal Appeal No. 55 of 2017, High
Court of Bombay at Goa, 2019.

quickly made his way home to make a call to the police.

At the Anjuna Police Station, Constable Gurunath Naik was manning the lines. Even in a coastal town with a happening nightlife, the beat police station officers expect most mornings to be relatively uneventful. An odd drunken driving crash or a post-party brawl is all they expect. At around 7.15 a.m., the phone buzzed and Gurunath Naik picked it up casually. The caller didn't wish to be identified but informed them about a body lying on the seashore. Soon they got a flurry of calls, all with the same information.

Naik, along with Police Constable Chandan and driver Vishant Chopdekar, proceeded to the spot to verify the call. He saw the body of a young girl lying in the shallow water that was splashing against her corpse. Gurunath later testified saying: 'There was nothing on her person except her brassiere which was on the right shoulder. The body was lying in a prone manner and the eyes and mouth were partly open.' He also noticed orange colour chappals at a distance of 2–3 m from the said body.

Gurunath Naik relayed the information back to the Anjuna Police Station, where Head Constable Krishna Naik made an entry in the station diary. He then proceeded to inform the Sub-Inspector Laxi Amonkar who in turn informed Inspector Nerlon Albuquerque.

Reshma Naik, a police constable, accompanied Laxi Amonkar to the Anjuna beach that morning. As curious onlookers gathered around, she lifted the bedsheet that now covered the body and examined the nude body. It was not a pleasant sight. The young girl had an abrasion on her left forehead and had grazed her knees. What stood out was her pierced lower lip, but besides that there were no noticeable external injuries.

Amonkar quickly completed formalities drawing up a *panchnama*. This is a mandatory legal document that enlists the details of the state in which the body was found. It also includes descriptions like mark of injuries found on the deceased; apparent cause of death; and the possible weapons that could have been used. The police then sent the body for the post-mortem examination. The autopsy was conducted that same afternoon.

At around 10.00 p.m., a grizzled, weather-beaten British woman walked into the Anjuna Police Station. She identified herself as Fiona Mackeown.

Fiona had been in Gokarna, a beach hideaway in the neighbouring state of Karnataka, when she received a message about her daughter. A devastated Fiona had hurried back to Goa. The following morning Fiona, along with a friend, went to the Goa Medical College and Hospital to identify the body. She confirmed that the body was of her third-born, Scarlett Keeling, only 15 years and eight months old.

∽

On 22 November 2006, when Fiona—along with her then partner Rob Clarke, a 47-year-old shopkeeper from the United Kingdom (UK)—came to Goa, she had felt a degree of freedom and a sense of accomplishment and relief. The six-month holiday that she had saved up for had finally begun.

Fiona lived with her family on a 9.5-acre smallholding in Bideford, Devon, where the family survived by rearing ponies, breeding puppies and growing their own food. Money wasn't easy to come by and she was living off benefits—a euphemism for doles handed out by the British government to citizens to make ends meet. A mother of nine children from four different men, Fiona's lifestyle had begun to bite (not that it bothered her).

It was her first trip to Goa—one that she had to sell a pony and save up her meagre earnings for. With eight of her nine children in tow, Fiona made the trip to India—partly for a change of scenery but more so because the family needed to escape the biting cold winters of England. Living in a creaking wooden cabin and some caravans in Bideford, her family could not handle the cold. The British currency, which seems meagre in Britain, goes a long way in India. Even the hashish that Fiona regularly smoked was easier to come by.

That morning, as she stood by the morgue cabinet of Scarlett, Fiona was coming to terms with her loss. 'It was horrific... I had a friend with me and both of us had to keep stopping because we were crying so much. Just... horrific,' Fiona said.[2]

Scarlett was a carefree teenager who loved partying and was fiercely independent. When the rest of the family made the trip from Goa to Gokarna, Scarlett stayed back saying she would be fine on her own. She was left in the care of Julio Lobo, a local guide. While she did travel to spend a week with her mum and siblings in Gokarna, barely a week before her death she insisted on returning to Goa.

The 25-year-old tout and guide Julio Lobo was her paramour. She had met him at a party in Anjuna beach

---

[2]Saner, Emine, '"I Can't Let Them Get Away With It"', *The Guardian*, 21 January 2009, https://tinyurl.com/mr2kjryr. Accessed on 7 June 2023.

in the third week of December. Her diary entries provide insight on the same. In an entry from 8 February 2008 she had noted:

> Dear Diary,
>
> I've been in India now for about two months and I've seen and experienced so much. But I'm stuk [sic]... At the full moon party I met this guy, Julio. I was pretty messed up, like I had taken a pill and drunk a lot of vodka. I don't remember a lot but apparently we had sex and I can remember that much but it took like two weeks b4 [before] me and Julio were hangin[g] out regularly.[3]

Julio, who was alternating between Goa (where he was born and raised) and Finland (where he used to work intermittently), later told the media that his relationship with Scarlett was 'something special'. While talking to the media after her death, he said: 'I really cared for her. Talking about love is out of the question now but I think we had something special together.' However, he was left exasperated by Scarlett's choices as 'she did what she wanted to do.'[4]

Fiona defended her decision to leave Scarlett behind, saying that allowing the teenager the freedom to chart her own way was a conscious choice. Fiona later said: 'Scarlett

---

[3]'EXCLUSIVE: Casual Sex, Drink and Drugs: The Disturbing Last Days of Murdered Schoolgirl Scarlett Revealed in Her Own Diary', *Evening Standard*, 13 April 2012, https://bit.ly/3BhdkrV. Accessed on 11 May 2023.

[4]'Scarlett's Indian boyfriend: Murdered Girl Had a Heavy Drink Problem- and Her Mother Knew all about It', *Evening Standard*, 13 April 2012, https://bit.ly/44SoJMc. Accessed on 11 May 2023.

was very independent... She was just like I was at her age. But my mother was very strict and that drove us apart for good. I wanted to have a more understanding relationship with Scarlett, and allowed her some freedom.'[5]

Scarlett's diary entries revealed that she was into consuming 'mushies' (hallucinogenic mushrooms), even back in England with her boyfriend Jardi. She described in her diary how she 'went to a party last night, got drunk, stoned and was trippin on mushies' before setting off for India. She also wondered how her relationship with Jardi would fare after six months apart. This diary entry was signed off as: 'SKAZ x'[6]

When talking to the media, Julio said: 'Scarlett had a drinking habit. She used to drink vodka, beer and tequila, sometimes in large amounts, and her mother knew this. When her family was away and she was with me, she'd be drunk many nights, so drunk she was falling over.'[7]

For Scarlett, the holiday proved to be a mix between enjoying her newfound freedom and pining for her life back home. After getting away from her family, she began to doubt Julio's intentions too. She wrote about how she missed Jardi and thought about him frequently. But she

---

[5]Henderson, Barney, and Caroline Davies, '"Why do They Attack Me? All I Want Is Justice for Scarlett"', *The Guardian*, 16 March 2008, https://bit.ly/3Blp0cY. Accessed on 11 May 2023.

[6]'EXCLUSIVE: Casual Sex, Drink and Drugs: The Disturbing Last Days of Murdered Schoolgirl Scarlett Revealed in her Own Diary', *Evening Standard*, 13 April 2012, https://bit.ly/3BhdkrV. Accessed on 11 May 2023.

[7]'Scarlett's Indian boyfriend: Murdered Girl Had a Heavy Drink Problem- and Her Mother Knew all about It', *Evening Standard*, 13 April 2012, https://bit.ly/44SoJMc. Accessed on 11 May 2023.

was conflicted, as she felt gratitude towards Julio for the support he had provided for her and her family. Julio was also supposed to take her to Finland. She doubted whether he really loved her or was just using her and feeling sorry for her. In her diary, she wrote: 'I want to go home.'[8]

Her final words in her diary were as follows: 'I rele rele rele [really, really, really] don't know what to do. I wish something big would happen to make my decision final.' This was accompanied by a doodle of a hangman.[9] (A premonition perhaps?)

On 17 February 2008 at about 2.00 p.m., Scarlett and Julio left for Curlies Bar. This is a shack at the southern end of Anjuna Beach, known for its happening nightlife. Julio and Scarlett would usually hang out there, playing pool or lounging. Between 4.00 p.m. and 5.00 p.m. that evening, Scarlett approached him saying that she wanted to buy some clothes, and the two left to go shopping. They returned to Curlies at around 6.00 p.m., where they hung out until 7.30 p.m. Scarlett also spoke to her mother from Julio's phone. Fiona informed her that they would be going back to England soon, to which Scarlett reacted with joy. This was the last conversation they had.

---

[8]'EXCLUSIVE: Casual Sex, Drink and Drugs: The Disturbing Last Days of Murdered Schoolgirl Scarlett Revealed in Her Own Diary', *Evening Standard*, 13 April 2012, https://bit.ly/3BhdkrV. Accessed on 11 May 2023.

[9]'The Disturbing Last Days of Murdered Schoolgirl Scarlett Revealed–Diary', *Daily Mail*, 16 March 2008, https://bit.ly/42qWLFU. Accessed on 11 May 2023.

Julio dropped Scarlett to a restaurant named Bean Me Up, where she was to meet her friend Ruby Caso, a Spanish girl whose family used to run Bean Me Up. She was to call Julio to pick her up when she was done. It was an evening like most others for them: a pub crawl, experimental drug use and getting smashed.

After an evening of drinking and drugs, Ruby and Scarlett parted ways at 12.30 a.m. Scarlett told Ruby that she would be making her way back to Siolim, where she was staying with Julio. Instead, for two hours, she wandered along the Anjuna Beach—a decision that did not serve her well.

For 29-year-old Samson D'Souza, this was to be a night like any other. A barman at Luis Café, he arrived at the shack between 2.30 p.m. to 3.00 p.m. after the afternoon crowd had fizzled out. He then manned the bar until the late hours of the night, often sitting well past 3.00 a.m. at the shack.

A typical Goan beach shack is around 18 m from back to front and 8 m wide. It is mainly set up using wood to drill stumps into the sand and build a planked floor, and dried coconut palms to create a thatched roof. The shack usually has tables and chairs arranged in restaurant style, a bar counter, a cash counter and a kitchen at the back. There is also often a pool table. Luis Café was a typical Goan beach shack replete with the decorative lights, potted plants and a music system. A few regular customers sat in the shack playing cards for hours, while smoking hashish and sniffing cocaine.

Samson usually had the company of Michael Manion

(Mike Masala), a carpenter from London holidaying in Goa and staying as a paying guest at Samson's house. Also accompanying them on most days was Placido Carvalho (Shanaboy), a small-time bookmaker for *matka* (a form of rural gambling popular in Goa and Maharashtra); and Murli Sagar, an employee of Curlies Bar. Murli used to hang out at Luis Café, sniffing coke and drinking beer during his time off.

That night, Murli Sagar completed his shift at Curlies at around 2.30 a.m. and by 2.40 a.m., he landed at Luis Café. He intended to spend time there until the wee hours. Upon entering the shack, he is said to have spoken briefly with the owner Luis Coutinho. He then proceeded to pick a beer from the bar counter and headed to the kitchen along with Shanaboy. They were also joined by Samson. Shanaboy then proceeded to uncover a plate with four lines of cocaine carefully laid out. Murli rolled up a currency note and sniffed one strip of cocaine, with Samson and Shanaboy following. Samson then returned to his place at the bar counter.

At around 3.00 a.m., Luis Coutinho was about to leave for home. He was just signalling to his staff the end of yet another day, when from the wooden steps of his shack he noticed someone lying on the beach. Noticing Luis looking at her, Scarlett got up and walked towards him unsteadily. Her gait was not normal and Luis first thought that she was drunk.

Scarlett, who could barely hold herself together, walked up to him and told him that she wanted to go to Anjuna. A bemused Luis told her that she was already in Anjuna. Scarlett then corrected herself, and told him that she wanted to go to Siolim. Coutinho asked her to hire a taxi from the market. Scarlett told him that she didn't have any money.

She then entered the shack and teetered towards the bar counter. She struck up a conversation with Samson, who was seated there, along with Mike Masala. She introduced herself and said it was her first time in Luis Café. She told them that she was a regular visitor at Curlies Bar. Samson offered her a beer, and asked if she knew anyone from Curlies.

Since Murli was seated at the back, Samson ushered her to the kitchen and introduced her to him. Murli instantly recognized her as the girl who used to regularly visit Curlies with her family. In his statement at the High Court, Murli described her as the girl who used to 'drink from the glasses left over by the other customers as she was fond of consuming alcohol'. Scarlett had clearly left a mark! He later told the police that he had seen her once or twice literally shaking under the influence of drugs.

Samson then returned to the bar counter while Scarlett remained in the kitchen, chatting with Shanaboy and Murli. Scarlett asked Murli if he had Julio's number, to which he responded with a no. She then asked him whether he could drop her to Julio's house. Since he didn't know where Julio stayed, he suggested that he could drop her to Curlies Bar.

Murli later testified and said:

At that time Scarlett moved towards Shana and sniffed one line of cocaine without asking anybody. At that time I was standing there, Shana was sitting and Samson was also standing. After sniffing the cocaine she sat down on the plastic chair and she was continuously talking and fumbling... My Kingfisher beer was on the table and Scarlett drank it without asking anybody.

Once outside the kitchen, Murli saw Mike Masala, who warned him that the girl had already consumed too much. Murli then went outside the shack to relieve himself. When he returned, he heard Mike Masala bellowing, 'How can these people give her Ecstasy?'

At this point, Luis tapped Murli on his shoulder to inform him that he was leaving. This was around 4.30 a.m. Shanaboy, Samson, Mike and Murli continued sitting at the shack with Scarlett present in their company.

Around that time, Murli received a text message from his girlfriend Katherine asking him about his whereabouts. Not looking forward to her wrath, he decided that it was time to head home. He asked Scarlett if she would like to come with him, so that he could drop her at Curlies. She agreed.

As he left the shack, Scarlett followed him and they walked towards the parking lot. However, Scarlett stopped midway, sat down in the sand and began talking about the stars. Getting impatient, Murli asked her again if she wanted to be dropped at Curlies but he got no response. Instead, he saw that Scarlett had laid down in the sand.

In his statement, Murli later said:

At that time, I saw Samson who came from the other side of the shack which also reached the parking area. I was surprised to see Samson as I had seen him at the bar counter talking with Masala and Shana. Samson told me to stay back and berated me for wanting to leave. [...] Scarlett then got up and ran towards a thicket. Samson also ran after her and caught her very firmly as she was out of control. Samson was coming back holding Scarlett from behind and I started my bike. At that time I realised that Scarlett was not in a condition to sit on my bike. Samson told me to go and that he would drop Scarlett.

Murli decided to leave. Samson informed him that Scarlett had lost her footwear and had asked him to search for it. He was, however, unsuccessful in doing so. Murli saw that Scarlett had sat down in the sand cross-legged with Samson, and it appeared to him that she was comfortable with him as she was relaxed and singing. It was the last time that he saw Scarlett.

After riding for about half a kilometre, he stopped to talk to his girlfriend on his mobile when Mike overtook him. He turned around and asked Murli about Scarlett. When Murli told him that Samson had promised to drop her, Mike was enraged and yelled at him saying: 'You don't know what's happening!' He then took a U-turn and sped off.

Mike later told the police that he witnessed Samson disrobing Scarlett while he lay on top of her, but he didn't intervene because there was no indication that the act wasn't consensual. After seeing this, Mike went to Samson's house but couldn't get in as he didn't have a key. Little did he know that as he waited for Samson, watching the first light filter through at dawn, Scarlett was already dead.

In his deposition to the police, Mike said: 'I was shocked and appalled because despite my informing Samson D'Souza and the others in the shack that the girl was a minor, he was assaulting her. I got on my scooter and drove away. But I was feeling rage at their actions against a minor girl.'

As they lay in the sand, Samson forced himself on Scarlett who was by then barely conscious. The alcohol, cocaine, ecstasy and possibly LSD had taken a heavy toll on her. Samson is said to have taken her towards the water, placed her on a sunbed near the water line and attempted to revive her.

There were no witnesses and Mike was the last to see the two together. Samson, who was arrested after the death became an international scandal, opted to exercise his right to remain silent.

Much later, the Inspector General of Police, Kishen Kumar, told the media: 'Scarlett passed out on the beach and Samson tried to revive her by splashing water on her face. She regained consciousness for a while and fainted again. At this juncture, Samson saw somebody approaching with a torchlight. He dumped her and fled.'[10]

Samson fled leaving Scarlett unconscious and naked at the beach, knowing very well that she would likely drown. He also left his orange flip-flops behind at the scene, which proved to be crucial in incriminating him.

❧

The next morning when Chandru Chavan, a waiter at Luis Café, woke up, he noticed something unusual. The lights in the shack were still blazing bright and the whisky

---

[10]Pereira, Andrew, and Preetu Nair, 'Rapist Confesses, Scarlett Case Solved: Cops', *The Times of India*, 14 March 2008, https://tinyurl.com/2k95u8em. Accessed on 27 July 2023.

glasses were on the counter. Usually, either Samson or Luis switched off the lights and placed the glasses in the kitchen before heading home. Chandru switched off the lights, and kept the glasses in place. He later testified that the previous night, when he had briefly woken up at around 4.30 a.m., he had seen Scarlett talking to Samson and Mike Masala at the bar counter.

As morning broke, a worried Julio began searching for Scarlett. When interacting with the media, Julio later said that she had told him that she would call when she was ready to be picked up. But when he didn't hear from her till morning, he went to look for her. Since there was no sign of her anywhere, he took his bike and went looking for her. He even asked people at the beach shacks if they had seen her. Much later that day, he was told that a body had been found at the beach. He soon found out that the body was Scarlett's. 'I couldn't believe it. I had seen her alive and in great form the evening before,' he said.[11]

A devastated Julio now had the onerous task of informing Fiona that Scarlett was dead. He contemplated calling Fiona on her mobile but could not muster the courage. At around 3.00 p.m., he sent her a message instead. Fiona quickly called back and Julio initially hesitated, only saying that something awful had happened to Scarlett and that she was in the hospital.

'Just tell me she is alive,' Fiona begged Julio over the phone. He just couldn't say yes.

---

[11]'Scarlett's Indian Boyfriend: Murdered Girl Had a Heavy Drink Problem–and Her Mother Knew All about It', *Evening Standard*, 13 April 2012, https://bit.ly/44SoJMc. Accessed on 11 May 2023.

Fiona left Gokarna at around 4.00 p.m. and reached Anjuna at about 10.00 p.m. and immediately went to the police station. There she was shown photographs of her daughter—photographs of what state she was found in that morning.

∽

The Goa Police initially closed the case as an accidental drowning, relying only on the autopsy report that noted sand and water in her lungs, along with other abrasions and injuries. Dr Silvano Sapeco, the head of the forensic department at the Goa Medical College and Hospital, conducted the first autopsy and declared death by drowning.

Fiona later said that she initially believed the police version despite knowing that Scarlett was a good swimmer. This was because she was told that Scarlett was seen intoxicated the previous night.

A day later, she visited Curlies and Luis Café to inquire whether anyone knew about the tragedy. When leaving from Luis Café, she was surprised to see her daughter's sandals, underwear and shorts lying along the beach. These were the first of a trail of breadcrumbs that ultimately pointed the way to a botched investigation.

In the glaring spotlight of the international media, a feisty Fiona accused politicians, including then Home Minister Ravi Naik, of trying to shield drug peddlers. She accused politicians of protecting assorted criminal gangs and of eliminating her daughter. This sent the Goa Police cowering for safety, and brought to the foreground the dark side of the best party destination in the country.

Inspector Nerlon Albuquerque, who initially asked the case to be closed as that of drowning, was suspended. He was replaced by Braz Menezes, who did the hard work of tracking down the case. It was later handed over to the Central Bureau of Investigation, all on account of media pressure.

The media pressure was such that it resulted in the involvement of foreign offices of the UK, along with ministers from the central level. With Fiona insisting that her daughter was murdered and owing to the pressure from the 24-hour news cycle, Dr Sapeco later added that while he was right in saying that Scarlett had died because of drowning, she could have been 'murdered with her head being forcefully held underwater until she drowned'. Later, in his court deposition, he said: 'The presence of bruises and abrasion on the body are suggestive of signs of struggle. The presence of alcohol and hypnotic drugs in blood are suggestive of a person is taken unaware or rendered senseless and defenceless by alcohol or hypnotic drug [and] the head is submerged in water for five to ten minutes.'

It was only due to Fiona's sustained questioning that the Goa administration ordered a second autopsy. This time, it was conducted by a panel of doctors. Her body was found to be intoxicated with cocaine and morphine, besides alcohol, in near fatal doses.

Samson faced trial for drugging, sexually assaulting and killing the 15-year-old Scarlett and thereafter trying to cover up his crimes. Shanaboy was accused of helping him drug her. Despite the doctors' testament, the investigators weren't able to establish that Samson wilfully and wittingly murdered Scarlett. This forced them to water down their charges to culpable homicide not amounting to murder, without the intent to kill. The charges of rape too were downgraded to molestation. The more serious charges of (first degree) murder against Samson were dropped. Samson in his defence in court claimed that he was 'wrongly framed and a case is created to enable the mother of the victim to receive monetary gains'.

It wasn't just Samson who was on trial. Soon, Fiona started being questioned. What was a teenage girl doing in the custody of an unfamiliar man, in an unfamiliar land while she herself was in a different part of the coast with her latest paramour? Pictures of her smoking from a hash pipe in the weeks preceding her daughter's death were also used to castigate her.

In an extensive interview with the *Daily Mail*, Fiona's former partner Rob Clarke—who separated with her during the course of her trip to India—accused her of wilfully neglecting her daughter. He said: 'She is in denial about her role in Scarlett's death. She could and should have prevented it. Every time, I tried to intervene, to keep Scarlett with the family and away from the drugs and party scene.' He added that all he received in return was a retort to mind his own business.[12]

Fiona's lawyer, Vikram Varma, dismissed Clarke's claims. He said that if Clarke had anything to say, he should do so as part of a deposition before the court.

The defendants too assailed Fiona. The advocate for the defendant Placido Carvalho (Shanaboy), said:

---

[12]'Inhaling Deeply from a Hash Pipe', *Mail Online*, 1 March 2009, https://tinyurl.com/4c5xcjfy. Accessed on 7 June 2023.

> How can she keep the custody of a minor girl with a stranger, very well knowing the fact that the person with whom the custody was kept was used to alcohol. So there was complete negligence on part of the mother of the deceased to take care of the custody of the child... Based on the evidence on record, there is clear evidence that the mother of the deceased girl was negligent in taking care of the child.

Fiona even faced a police case with a social activist, Aires Rodrigues, who accused her of neglecting Scarlett. But Fiona braved it all.

Eleven years after her daughter met her end on the sands of Anjuna Beach, and three years after the heartbreak of seeing the court acquit Samson and Shanaboy of charges, the light at the end of the tunnel was near for Fiona. Shanaboy had been charged with supplying drugs, intoxicating and conspiring to kill Scarlett.

On 17 July 2019, reporters jostled for space with men in long dark robes in the narrow video conference room of the High Court of Bombay at Goa. The High Court had completed a nearly two-year process of hearing arguments against the earlier acquittal granted by the trial court, and had finally arrived at a conclusion.

In one corner of the room sat a bearded Samson D'Souza dressed in a checked shirt with rolled-up sleeves, nervously fidgeting with his thumbs. Besides him sat Shanaboy (who was now emaciated, with drug abuse having clearly taken a toll on his once robust physique). Judge Prithviraj Chavan walked into the courtroom a little after 3.00 p.m., while Judge R.D. Dhanuka joined the proceedings via video conference.

Samson D'Souza was pronounced guilty on all counts of narcotizing, sexually assaulting and ultimately held responsible for the death of the 15-year-old Scarlett.

The High Court observed:

> He had prepared the plan in his mind to lure the victim so he could exploit her sexually and thereafter made her consume beer and intoxicant... Samson not only made the victim consume the liquor but also allowed her to sniff cocaine which had resulted in the victim totally inebriated under the influence as is evident from the medical evidence.

The High Court further noted: 'Lasciviousness of Samson is writ large.' He was sentenced to 10 years in prison and was ordered to pay a fine of nearly ₹250,000. This was handed over to Fiona as compensation for her great loss. Samson's pleas of being a reformed man, now saddled with responsibilities of raising his own kids, were ignored by the High Court.

Immediately after the verdict was announced, Fiona said: 'It's been so long that it is taking time for all of it to sink in. We didn't know it would ever come to this.'[13]

---

[13]'Convict in Scarlett Keeling Case Sentenced to 10-Yr Jail', *Hindustan Times*, 20 July 2019, https://tinyurl.com/34dznvf7. Accessed on 11 July 2023.

However, Fiona's travails didn't end. In 2010, she was sentenced to eight months in prison for falsely claiming £19,000 in income support. But the Exeter Crown Court suspended her jail term after hearing that she may lose her home in order to repay the debt.[14]

Two days before Scarlett's death, Fiona's eldest son, Halloran Keeling (Hal) was hit by a car on 15 February 2008. However, he survived by a grim chance. Fiona claimed that Hal could never overcome his sister's death, and passed away after a fatal overdose of morphine in 2017.

Samson vowed that he would challenge his conviction in the Supreme Court. As of now, he is serving his sentence.

---

[14]"Scarlett Mother Fiona Mackeown May Lose Her Devon Home", *BBC*, 1 March 2011, https://tinyurl.com/c5yut5n3. Accessed on 11 July 2023.

4

FROM THE FRYING PAN AND INTO THE FIRE

How a bowl of mutton soup revealed a murder

He's the most dangerous and brilliant criminal mind I've ever known. For years I've been watching him, tracking him, studying his every move. I know his every mannerism, facial tick, gesture. I know him better than he knows himself and now after all this time I've figured out a way to trap him. I will become him.[1]

This dialogue of Sean Archer, a special FBI Agent in the movie *Face/Off*, was perhaps lost in translation when Vamshi Paidipally (a Telugu film director) decided to make a Telugu version of the highly rated Hollywood film.

The carefully crafted Hollywood version sees Sean Archer, a character first played by John Travolta and later Nicolas Cage, 'exchange' his face with a dreaded terrorist Castor Troy.

---

[1]'Face/Off', *Quotes.net*, https://tinyurl.com/29z84vzj. Accessed on 13 July 2023.

He does this in order to penetrate the terror ring, and to get his accomplices to tell him crucial details about the location of a bomb. *Face/Off* went on to become a blockbuster, earning critical acclaim for its acting performances (especially for Cage and Travolta), stylized action sequences and for John Powell's musical score. It had emotional depth, originality, humour, great direction and stunts.

Vamshi Paidipally's Telugu remake titled *Yevadu* retained only the face-exchange premise. It then weaved a long-winded and complicated story around that premise involving lovers, the underworld, politicians and lots of fist fights. But lost in the melee was the effort their Hollywood counterparts had put into the changing of roles.

This was a film that M. Swathi Reddy and her paramour Ajjakolu Rajesh had watched with keen intent.

∽

The 24-year-old physiotherapist, Rajesh, had life going his way. He was a qualified medical practitioner with a secure job. He had good looks to complement a fairly built frame, and a decent bank balance to complete the package. By the reckoning of most, he was a dashing young man. It was no surprise that he would find no shortage of suitors. However, the one who caught his eye was a married woman who was also his patient.

Swathi Reddy, a trained nurse, lived in Nagarkurnool (in Telangana). From the outside, it seemed like she had a happy married life. The 27-year-old was a mother of two, and first met Rajesh during her physiotherapy sessions after her second pregnancy. Her husband, Sudhakar Reddy, was a civil contractor. His job was enough to provide for the family, and also enough for them to buy a Maruti Suzuki Brezza (a compact SUV that is out of reach even for most upper middle-class families).

Swathi's affair with Rajesh began in the clinic. Along with getting her back in shape, the young physiotherapist was also tugging the strings of her heart. The more she met him, the more she liked him. Before they knew it, the two had exchanged phone numbers and were texting each other for hours on end.

Later in a *Times of India* interview, the Nagarkurnool Deputy Superintendent of Police (DSP) Lakshmi Narayana said: 'Rajesh and Swati had an affair for two years and Rajesh would often visit Swati's home in the absence of her husband. They would speak on the phone at least five times a day. Sudhakar was busy with business and had little time for his wife.'[2]

Soon, the affair grew to such an extent that it could only go further if unshackled from its 'illicit' nature. Rajesh was eager to start a new life together, but Swathi's husband Sudhakar was an obstacle to this plan. Rather than eloping, as Rajesh wanted, Swathi chose a different route.

In a conservative society that dominates large parts of India, eloping is easier said than done. A woman can't just leave her husband and walk away if she's found somebody new. Heck, she can't even walk away if her husband is mistreating

---

[2]Reddy, U. Sudhakar, 'Night of Horror Before Mutton Soup Gave Away Murder Plot', *The Times of India*, 16 December 2017, https://bit.ly/3TBVJmZ. Accessed on 24 March 2023.

her. A woman can never walk away without incurring the wrath of society and facing ostracism.

Swathi's problem was even bigger than that. Not only was she married to a rather well-to-do man but she had also mothered two kids, whose custody she had no hope of retaining if she walked away. Maybe she felt cornered and knew that she could not even count on the support of her own parents were she to leave. She didn't want to leave her children behind, and taking them along with her must have seemed out of the question. She had to think out of the box.

Maybe Swathi and Rajesh should have paid more attention to the details when they, after much deliberation, decided on a plan. The two lovers came up with the most outrageous plan modelled on the plot of *Face/Off* as seen in *Yevadu*. Yes, they had decided they would attempt to foolishly pull off what was shown in the movies. Their plan was much more sinister and evil compared to the movie. It involved the murder of Sudhakar, followed by Rajesh pretending to be Sudhakar and living the rest of his life as him. For some reason, they thought they would get away with it. Perhaps, it was the desperation of the situation that drove them to this. If not for their callous lack of attention to detail, maybe they could have taken the charade a little further.

They ruminated over it for three months and finalized their plan. They planned to kill Sudhakar and get rid of his body. Then Swathi would 'gently' burn Rajesh's face with acid and petrol, in a bid to disguise him. Later, Rajesh was to go through plastic surgery to treat his burns. Any difference in resemblance with the real Sudhakar would be blamed on the plastic surgery, and they would then live happily ever after. Or so they thought!

The DSP later said, 'She plotted to eliminate him and sent her two children to her parents' house in Telkapally, days before the murder.'[3]

❧

On 26 November 2017, Swathi and Rajesh strangulated Sudhakar and battered him with a wooden log. However, he survived the attack. Their plan was foiled. They shifted the unsuspecting man to a hospital, where he was discharged within a few hours. Swathi claimed that Sudhakar had injured himself in a fall.

A confused Sudhakar couldn't recall the fall, but he blamed it on the injury. He called his cousin, Aravind, to stay over for the night. Maybe, he suspected that the 'fall' might happen again.

Swathi asked Aravind to leave in the early hours, and called Rajesh home to re-enact their sinister plan.

On 27 November 2017, Swathi injected her husband with an anaesthetic. As soon as it took effect, the duo struck Sudhakar with a blunt object on the back of his head. They made sure that he was dead, dragged his body to a remote part of the wilderness and set it ablaze, leaving it partially burnt.

Swathi then smeared Rajesh's face with petrol and acid. Rajesh was a willing participant in the plan. All this, just for 'love'.

❧

---

[3]Ibid.

As was planned, Swathi raised the alarm. Later, Investigation Officer Srinivas Rao said, 'She called up Sudhakar's parents and told them that four persons entered their house and attacked Sudhakar. Although they expressed their doubts that it does not appear to be their son, they agreed to shift him to Apollo Hospital in Hyderabad as Swathi insisted that he immediately needed plastic surgery.'[4]

Initially, the in-laws bought the ruse. In the dim light of dawn, they rushed who they thought was Sudhakar to a private hospital. There he was given the necessary first aid and a plastic surgery to repair the burns on his face.

Both Swathi and Rajesh played their respective roles feigning distress. Obviously, in Rajesh's case it was actual distress. They were braced to endure what they thought would be a brief storm of awkward questions from relatives. They believed that they could resume their lives after that, now as husband and wife. But things didn't seem to be going according to their plan.

Rajesh, despite claiming to be getting better, refused to speak and only gestured to the relatives in response to their questions. Rather than speaking, 'Sudhakar' would offer to write down his responses. He may have looked somewhat like Sudhakar, but things appeared odd to the relatives. They were constantly at his bedside and probably wanted to stay there until he got well. For starters, Rajesh was shorter than Sudhakar—something that would be apparent to anyone. In an effort to conceal the differences,

---

[4]Janyala, Sreenivas, 'Telangana: Woman Disfigures Lover's Face to Pass Him off as Murdered Husband', *The Indian Express*, 13 December 2017, https://bit.ly/3nbb29P. Accessed on 24 March 2023.

Rajesh used to ask for the lights in his hospital room to be dimmed. He would also pretend to be asleep most of the day, especially when a particularly nosy relative came to see him.

There were other things too that didn't add up. The 'new' Sudhakar couldn't recognize any of the relatives who called on him, nor could he name close family members. Maybe that is when the family's list of doubts began to grow.

Things came to a head when he refused to have a bowl of mutton soup being served to patients at the hospital. Rajesh was a vegetarian. The real Sudhakar was not just fond of meat-based foods, he would have possibly killed to get hold of some. And yet here he was, refusing a bowl of steaming hot mutton soup!

Either Sudhakar's facial scars had changed his personality forever, or the man lying on the bed was not him. All it took was 24 hours for Sudhakar's brother to lodge a police complaint, alleging that the man lying on the hospital bed was an imposter. This was after the family had coughed up ₹5 lakh for the plastic surgery. Preliminary investigations revealed that the fingerprints taken from the person at the hospital didn't match those recorded in the Aadhaar database for Sudhakar Reddy.

∽

Swathi's days of freedom were over. She quickly buckled under pressure from investigators and admitted to having murdered her husband with Rajesh's help. She also guided the police to the location of the body. Police retrieved the partially burned and decomposed body, and handed it over to the family members.

Swathi and Rajesh were promptly booked for murder, but Rajesh was to be arrested only after he was discharged from the hospital. Within two weeks, he was discharged and promptly arrested. He broke down and passed the buck to Swathi for having planned the murder. 'Swati was not happy with Sudhakar. So, she got close to me,' Rajesh told reporters upon his arrest.[5] In his defence, Rajesh claimed that the entire plan was hatched by Swathi who rejected the prospect of eloping. She was keen on having her children with her, and also wanted to stay in touch with her parents. Swathi had feared she would have to leave behind more than she could bear. She found it unimaginable for her children to feel abandoned. She must have feared that with eloping came the reality of leaving her old life behind, especially her parents.

As soon as the murder came to light, her parents announced that they had disowned their daughter. Her father even symbolically conducted her funeral rituals, indicating their displeasure to the rest of the village. When Swathi was offered the option of bail pending the trial, no one from her family came forward to help her secure the bail bonds or to offer surety on her behalf. Even 10 days after being allowed bail, she remained in prison. While there were well-meaning persons who came forward to offer her surety, she refused. She was holding out hope that at least someone from her family would relent. Finally, Swathi was given bail through the efforts of the State Legal Services Authorities. She was then moved to a shelter for women.

∞

---

[5]'Telangana Murder Case: Accused A. Rajesh arrested', *Mumbai Mirror*, 14 December 2017, https://bit.ly/3FPyyjb. Accessed on 24 March 2023.

In a society in which family honour is placed way above individual freedom, it should really have come as no surprise that no one chose to come forward to help her. The tone was already set to indicate that it was Swathi who was the prime accused in the case. She was the one who coerced Rajesh into her evil plan—not quite unlike how Eve had 'tempted' Adam into taking a bite of the forbidden fruit.

'It was Swathi's plan to eliminate her husband and live with Rajesh along with her kids,' the Nagarkurnool police said soon after they completed their preliminary investigations.[6]

Swathi was also denied the chance to meet her children, who were now being cared for by their maternal grandparents. Her whole life crumbled around her. Swathi and Rajesh may never get to see each other again—that's assuming they even want to. Things appeared to have broken down between them, as a blame game played out before the eyes of the media.

Mutton soup or not, it was unlikely that the plan would have ever succeeded. Yet, one cannot help but wonder what might have happened had the duo taken a little bit more trouble to pay attention to the details. Would Rajesh have gotten away had he gleefully accepted the mutton soup? Would all differences and odd behaviour be convincingly blamed on the burn injuries? And what about his voice?

One can't help but wonder what might have happened if Swathi and Rajesh would have been hooked on the *Mission Impossible* franchise instead. They would have perhaps just used a mask then.

---

[6]'Mutton Soup Thickens: Duo Attacked Sudhakar Earlier Too', *The New Indian Express*, 16 December 2017, https://tinyurl.com/ms4t5pun. Accessed on 7 June 2023.

5

THE AIR HOSTESS SUICIDE
THAT WASN'T

*The murder and deception of aspiring
air hostess Shashi Roy*[1]

On 29 March 2008, two boys rushed into Sahi Hospital
(Nizamuddin in New Delhi) at 10.45 a.m. with a
grievously injured girl. She was bleeding profusely and had
deep gashes on her neck and abdomen. She had attempted
suicide, the two boys told Jyoti Rambert, the administrator of
the hospital. They said they were her cousins, and identified
themselves as Vishal Chaudhary and Manoj Chaudhary.
The scene at the multi-storey hospital quickly turned grim
and frantic, as doctors battled to save her life. The woman
brought to the hospital was Shashi Roy.

Dr Leena Dadhwal, a surgeon at the hospital, was the
first to examine her. What she saw made her realize that
she had no time to waste. There was a 12-cm-long cut

---

[1]Case details and quotations from: Ashish Nandwana v. State,
CRL.A.269/2012, Delhi High Court, 1 September 2014.

near the upper fold in the neck. It was so deep that it had cut through her trachea, puncturing a hole right into her airway. Two deep, lacerated wounds slashed through her abdomen just below the ribs and even pierced a few vital organs (including her liver, gallbladder and small intestine).

While the girl was conscious, she couldn't speak since her voice box was cut. This forced the doctors to ask Manoj and Vishal to sign the consent form, even as she was rushed into the operating room. The duo dutifully did so.

Dr Dadhwal and her team quickly got to work. The doctors performed a high-risk surgery plugging the bleeding arteries, repairing the perforations of the liver and small intestine. They even administered six bottles of blood to help cope with the blood loss, and hooked her up to a ventilator, hoping for the best.

But many questions were arising. The Chaudhurys had claimed that it was a suicide attempt. But the injuries didn't add up. After all, how often does one hear of a person attempting suicide by stabbing themselves in the neck and stomach? That's the stuff of old Bollywood drama. Suicide attempts in real life tend to be less messy, with incidents of even wrist slashing being extremely rare.

At around 2.30 p.m., the hospital administrators decided that they shouldn't take chances and that it would be best to inform the police. The Hazrat Nizamuddin Police Station dispatched a team led by a sub-inspector to the hospital, after registering a case. But by then, too much time had elapsed and doctors declared her unfit to give a statement. Owing to this, crucial evidence was lost. Her 'cousins', Manoj and Vishal, were nowhere to be seen.

At 6.45 p.m., Shashi Roy was declared dead. All of 23

years and on the cusp of a career as an air hostess, Shashi Roy's life was brutally cut short just as it was about to take off.

The focus quickly shifted to the police. Local inquiries made by the police revealed that the girl had been brought to the hospital from Central Guesthouse, a stone's throw away from the hospital.[2] The police made their way there. Upon checking the register, they walked into room No. 232, only to find to their horror that the walls were splattered with blood; the bedsheets were soaked in the deep maroon hues of dried blood; and things lying all over the place. Nothing about the scene hinted at a suicide attempt. The police quickly upgraded the case to murder and the inquiry began.

The Nizamuddin area of Delhi is a bustling centre of activity. The neighbourhood is flanked on one side by the impressive tomb of Mughal emperor Humayun, and on other by the railway junction. It offers a mix of the regalia of the well-maintained archaeological marvels, along with the realities of an otherwise mid-to-low-income neighbourhood.

Home to the Nizamuddin railway station—where several long-distance trains begin and end their journey—the lanes and bylanes are bustling with travellers visiting the area for religious reasons and people on the lookout for budget accommodation (sometimes only for a few hours). The Central Guesthouse at Basti Nizamuddin was one such guest house that offered hourly accommodation.

[2]Singh, Vijaita, '2 Held for Aspiring Airhostess' Murder', *Hindustan Times*, 1 April 2008, https://bit.ly/3ZgxHzO. Accessed on 2 March 2023.

It was past 2.00 a.m. when two couples—Ashish Nandwana and Shashi Roy; and Manoj Kumar Nandwana (Ashish's cousin) and Savita Gupta (Savi)—drove up to the gates of Central Guesthouse. The four of them, all aged 23 at the time, were on the cusp of their careers. Shashi and Savita were studying at the Frankfinn Institute of Air Hostess Training in Jaipur, and hoped they would land jobs soon.

Hailing from Ranchi and the daughter of a practising criminal lawyer, Shashi had moved to Jaipur in the hope that the Jaipur branch of Frankfinn would offer better prospects than the one in her own hometown. Jaipur was a city that drew tourists, including foreigners, by the thousands, and offered greater exposure to those wishing to join the airline industry. It was quite unlike Ranchi, which wasn't exactly a hub of air traffic.

Ashish was an undergraduate and son of a businessman based in Jaipur. He helped his father run his business. His cousin Manoj worked as an assistant security officer at Deccan Airways in Jaipur.

Shashi was a fun-loving girl, and liked to frequent nightclubs in Jaipur. It was at one such nightclub that she had met Ashish and they had become friends. Soon, the two became more than just friends.

Early 2008 saw many highs for India. The global financial crisis was still months away from sending shockwaves throughout the world economy, and things were still looking positive, especially in India. A bunch of low-cost carriers had just launched operations in the country, and the likes of Vijay Mallya were the poster boys of a new and emerging India—one that was not risk-averse.

This was an India where youngsters—who saw the economic reforms unleash a new wave of foreign content and products upon impressionable minds—were only just becoming adults. Having grown up on a diet of cable TV, Western serials and mannerisms, these youngsters were now ready to take on the world. They were a far cry from their parents, whose generation was decidedly more conservative. The prejudices that held the previous generations back were being dropped, especially when these youngsters were out of their parents' sight.

Shashi was living with relatives in Jaipur while she studied, but believed that life was not 'all work and no play'. Her classmate Savita, who hailed from Jodhpur in Rajasthan, would also join her on her visits to party clubs and city hotspots (where people their age would hang out). Savita met Manoj through Shashi, and the four were soon double dating and hanging out together.

With her course in Jaipur nearing an end, Shashi was hoping to ultimately get a job and move to Delhi.

∽

On 24 March 2008, five days before her death, Shashi had called her parents. Shashi's distraught father, Pramod Kumar Roy, later said: 'Shashi had called me on March 24 from Jaipur, saying that she was going to Gurgaon for an interview. On reaching Gurgaon, Shashi called me again from a PCO. [...] That was the last time I heard from my daughter.'[3] After giving several job interviews in Delhi,

---

[3]Tripathi, Rahul, 'Father Vows to Get Daughter Justice', *The Times of India*, 1 April 2008, https://tinyurl.com/4fp75afv. Accessed on 7 June 2023.

Shashi was supposed to head back to Ranchi.

Manoj, Ashish and Savi left for Delhi in Ashish's Indica on 28 March 2008. Shashi joined them from Behror (on the way between Rajasthan and Delhi). The drive from Jaipur was a good five-hour journey without any stopovers.

It was only when they reached Delhi that they realized that they also needed a place to stay. That was not easy to come by, as unmarried couples booking hotel rooms were not welcome and often received a harsh response from people. Getting a hotel, that too well past midnight, turned out to be much more difficult than they had originally thought.

Shashi turned to her local friend Mohammed Dilshad to try and arrange a room for them. They picked Dilshad from the area around India Gate. He then took them to the Central Guesthouse. Sahid Siddique (the manager of the guest house) initially refused to let them stay. It was only after Dilshad assured that they would provide a guarantee that he relented. Even then there was the condition that the girls would sleep in one room and the boys in another.

It was well past two when the four of them finally settled in for the night after completing formalities. These formalities included Ashish and Dilshad giving copies of their identity cards for the hotel record, and the rest of them entering their names in the register. Savita, who hailed from a conservative family, entered her name on the register as Julie.

Despite assurances of the boys and girls sleeping separately, they had no intention of keeping their word. Siddique, the manager of the guest house, later testified before the police that he saw Shashi and Ashish staying together in room No. 232 and Julie and Manoj stay in room No. 233.

So far, it all seemed fine. They were just young adults from conservative families exploring the frontiers of adulthood, without the supervision of elders. They were making the most of their newfound freedom. But all was not well.

Shashi had apparently spent Holi with some male friends back in Jaipur, without Ashish. This did not go down well with him. A few days prior, Shashi was in the company of 'other boys', and the fact that she stayed with them from 23–28 March without telling Ashish soon became a bone of contention.

Shashi also harboured simmering discontent with Ashish. She had spurned his marriage proposals on more than one occasion. Even after he had approached her family to state the seriousness of his intent, she had refused to budge. She had astutely told him that there was no question of her saying yes to his proposal, as he was an alcoholic as well as unemployed.

Shashi's father later told the media that his daughter had confided in him that Ashish was a source of trouble.[4] He had then prompted her to try and avoid Ashish. The father claimed that Ashish even approached him, as many as three times, seeking her hand in marriage.

Even with all this, there they were sharing a room at a budget hotel in Delhi. The guest house staff later claimed that the two seemed fine and behaved like a married couple.

✌

[4]'Death Shock before Job Result', *The Telegraph online*, 1 April 2008, https://tinyurl.com/ydfyrmdm. Accessed on 27 July 2023.

But things came to a head in Room No. 232. As night turned to dawn, things took a turn for the worse. The couple had a bitter fight over the fact that Shashi had rejected Ashish's proposals, and was so friendly with other men. The simmering anger and her honesty in expressing her objections must have left Ashish filled with rage, jealousy, indignation and a sense of humiliation. He just couldn't stomach that a young and independent woman, determined to chart her own path, could say no to him. How dare she? How dare she have a mind of her own?

Engulfed by his rage, his feelings got the better of him. Ashish first tried to smother her but was unsuccessful. This left prominent fingernail scratches across her face and neck. He then pulled out a knife (that he had carried with him), and stabbed her first on her neck and then repeatedly in her abdomen. Shashi screamed in pain but soon went silent, as Ashish ripped open her voice box.

Hearing her cries, Manoj came to their room. When he entered the room, he saw blood splattered all over and Shashi losing consciousness. Rather than trying to help the victim, Manoj helped Ashish wash off the blood. The duo panicked and poured water on Shashi to make it look like an accident. Scared that other guests may have also heard the cries, and with little time to think their strategy through, they decided to fabricate a story. They said that Shashi had fallen in the bathroom and ended up seriously hurting herself.

A little later, Savi joined them. The boys told her that Shashi had had a bad fall in the bathroom. The three began to panic, with Savi panicking the most. She must have felt that her moral reputation was at stake. How could she tell her parents that she had slept in a room with a boy? She later faked a story that she was sleeping in the room with Shashi but had gone to the other room to take a bath. Manoj too found himself in a messy situation, confronted with this crime and his loyalty to Ashish.

After inquiring with the guest house staff about a nearby hospital, they wrapped Shashi in a bedsheet and took her to the Sahi Hospital.

As previously mentioned, at the hospital Ashish gave his name as Vishal Chaudhury and Manoj called himself Manoj Chaudhury. They told the hospital staff that it was a suicide attempt. But to everyone else, including Dilshad, they said that Shashi had injured herself in the bathroom. Ashish and Manoj even asked Dilshad to lend them some money.

Dilshad was already uncomfortable with the situation, since he had put his own reputation at stake by offering a guarantee for Shashi and her friends. Owing to this, he bluntly refused to lend them the money. But an unflinching Ashish insisted that Dilshad at least come to the hospital.

Dilshad went with a friend to Sahi Hospital and met Ashish and Manoj in the waiting room. Upon inquiring, he was told that everything was fine and that the doctor only wanted some blood to be arranged. Dilshad, being the ever-resourceful guy, not only arranged for blood but also donated blood before leaving. It was only later that evening that Dilshad realized that something was amiss. He received a phone call from the Station House Officer asking him to visit the police station, in order to record his statement.

༄

Ashish and Manoj thought they had done just about enough to save themselves. But now came the big question—what was next for them? Was it in their interest if she survived or was it better that she didn't? After all, dead people tell no tales and it was only the two of them who witnessed what happened in Room No. 232 that morning.

They ended up doing what most criminals would do. It was time to end the charade. Without waiting to know if Shashi would survive, they sneaked out of the hospital; came back to the guest house at around 12.30 p.m.; collected their car and belongings; and checked out. The two dropped off Savi at India Gate, from where she went on to catch a bus to Jaipur from the Inter-State Bus Terminus. The men took a train from Nizamuddin and abandoned their car at the Hazrat Nizamuddin Railway Station.

To their credit, the Delhi Police acted quickly. From the register at the guest house, the police recovered the names of those who had occupied those two rooms that night. From the consent form at the hospital, they recovered the names and phone numbers of the 'cousins' who had admitted Shashi to the hospital.

It didn't take the experienced police force much time to put two and two together and realize what had transpired. While Ashish and Manoj were smart enough to give false identities while admitting Shashi to the hospital, they were stupid enough to give a real mobile number on the consent form for the surgery. As per the records of Tata Teleservices, the phone number had no clear name but the registered address was the same as Ashish's Jaipur address.

By 7.30 p.m. the same day both Ashish and Manoj were arrested and the knife, which Ashish had dumped in a gutter along Mathura Road, was recovered. The car was seized and blood stains from the car were examined by forensic experts, as the police began to painstakingly build a case.

ॐ

On 24 December 2011, after a three-year trial, the Additional Sessions Judge convicted Ashish for the offence of murder and destroying evidence pertaining to the crime. The co-accused, Manoj, was acquitted of the charge of murder but was convicted for the offence of destroying evidence. Both of them were acquitted of the charge of conspiracy.

They made one last-ditch attempt to extricate themselves from the crime and to try and convince the trial court of their innocence. Not only did Ashish and Manoj plead not guilty of having murdered Shashi, they also cooked up a story about a fall in the bathroom on shards of glass. They used this to explain how she had sustained her injuries. To prove their story, they even convinced Shahid Siddique and Mohammed Siddique (a room attendant of the guest house) to testify in their favour. They said that they saw Shashi walking down the stairs towards the reception covering her neck with her scarf, claiming she had been injured in a fall. They then said that she inquired about the nearest hospital. To further defend the boys, they even added for good measure that Ashish and Manoj were not in the guest house when Shashi injured herself but were out having breakfast and tea.

Shahid Siddique's deposition said:

> At 8:30 AM the girls called the attendant for tea to be served and since there was no kitchen facility in

the guest house they were told that they could take tea outside the guest house. Thereafter Ashish and Manoj came to me and enquired about availability of tea. I told them that they could take tea outside the guest house after which the boys left.

He then claimed that an attendant told him that a girl had fallen in room No. 232. He added that 10–15 minutes after Ashish and Manoj had stepped out from the guest house, Shashi came to his counter, pressing a scarf to her neck.

Shahid Siddique later told the court:

> I asked what had happened. She replied that she had fallen in the bathroom and sustained injuries. She inquired whether there was a hospital nearby. I asked her whether the injuries were serious and she replied that it was a minor injury. I told her about Shahi Hospital. Ashish and Manoj came back in the meanwhile and took her to Shahi Hospital.

Mohammed Siddique too recalled a similar story. He testified that the girls stayed in one room and the boys in the other. He further added:

> The next morning the girls rang up from room No. 232 asking for tea to be served. I told them that the kitchen facility was not available and they could go outside to take tea. Thereafter I saw Ashish and Manoj leaving the guest house to take breakfast. Soon thereafter one girl came down holding her neck and abdomen...she informed that she had sustained injuries when she fell on pieces of glass. In the meanwhile, Ashish and Manoj came back and took the injured girl to the hospital,

but before leaving the girl told the Manager that her room and bathroom should be cleaned.

These testimonies were clearly a cover-up operation. There was a glaring hole in their version of events. The statements vastly differed from what they had first told the investigating officers. They had previously told the police that the boys and girls did not sleep separately. They had also said that Shashi was carried, wrapped in a bedsheet, by Ashish and Manoj. They had even said that when they asked what had happened, Ashish had told them that Shashi had fallen in the bathroom. Along with this, these testimonies were patently false for one other obvious reason. As the High Court noted, 'Shashi was not in a position to speak because the subcutaneously deep [injury] on both sides of the trachea had cut the muscle up to the trachea. The thyroid cartilage was cut.'

The High Court judges pointed to the deposition by Dr Leena Dadhwal. She testified that the patient could not speak as her voice box was cut. This was a testimony that remained unchallenged during cross examination.

The Delhi High Court, which heard the appeal by Ashish Nandwana against his conviction, said:

It may be true that Dr Leena Dadhwal had said that Shashi was conscious when she was brought to the hospital, but has clarified that she was not in a position to speak. The issue is not Shashi's consciousness. It is one of Shashi being in a position to speak. We note that Shashi's post mortem report also corroborates that her voice pin box has a hole [...] This completely demolishes the defence which is premised on the unfortunate fact of giving a twist to the truth, obviously being won over by the accused, to justify a defence which has no foundation: a defence which is a castle built with sand on sand near the sea beach, a gentle wave capable of sweeping away which airy castle.

Also, if Shashi fell on glass, why weren't there any glass pieces found in the room or anything made of glass that was missing from the room? The crime team, summoned for a forensic examination of the room, did not find broken pieces of glass anywhere. Pertinently, no corresponding cuts resulting from the alleged fall over broken glass were found on the clothes of the deceased. The post-mortem report also noted that the injury was so deep inside the body that it was impossible for a glass piece to do such damage.

It wasn't just the guest house owner and attendant who were won over by the accused. At one point, even the doctors were won over by them. The High Court was especially scathing of the opinion rendered by Dr Leena Dadhwal and Dr Siva Prasad. The High Court said that they have 'spoken a white lie when they admitted the suggestion that the injuries could be suffered by Shashi if she fell on a glass'. The High Court further noted, 'It is apparent that Dr. Leena Dadhwal and Dr. Siva Prasad have been won over by the accused. We are left aghast at the murky depth to which humans can fall. The two are ready to stake their careers for money.'

Ashish Nandwana was sentenced to life in prison and is currently serving sentence at Tihar jail in New Delhi. Manoj was sentenced for three years and then walked free. He chose not to challenge his conviction, as he had already served the term of his sentence when the verdict was announced.

For Shashi's family, life will never be the same again. Her father later said, 'I had told her to bear with him for some more days till the course was over. But now I regret that decision.' He later told *The Telegraph*, 'She was planning to come back to Ranchi after attending interviews in Delhi. As her training was complete, I told her to wait until she got a job.'[5]

The conviction of Ashish and Manoj was little relief to the family who would never see their daughter again—the daughter whose promising life was snuffed out by a man unwilling to stomach a rejection.

---

[5]Ibid.

6

IDLIS, DOSAS, MURDER

*The murder of Prince Santhakumar by
'Dosa King' Pitchai Rajagopal*[1]

The monsoon is both the best and the worst time to be patrolling the ghats of the Kodaikanal range in Tamil Nadu. The ghats are wet, and full of leeches and other dangerous life forms—lying in wait behind the thick forest growth. But it is also a time when forest life is blooming in its full glory, when all forms of life are happy and unafraid to make themselves known. For any forester worth his weight in salt, this is the ideal time to be patrolling the forests.

It was 31 October 2001. Forester Raman and Forest Guard Murugusen were on their rounds as usual, looking out for any signs of encroachers, loggers, hunters, poachers and other mischievous elements. But what they found that day took them by surprise, even though it would be months before

[1]Quotations and case details from: P. Rajagopal v. The Inspector of Police, C.A. No. 637 and 748 of 2004, M.P. No. 164 of 2008, Madras High Court, 19 March 2009.

the real importance of their find became apparent to them.

The pair came across the sprawling body of a youngish man. He appeared to have been dumped there—this was no trekking trip gone wrong but a beaten and bruised body. It was an attempt to conceal what was obviously a murder.

Raman and Murugusen quickly reported what they had seen to the Kodaikanal Police Station, under whose jurisdiction the area fell. The police, recording the finding of an unidentified body and its unnatural death, sent it for a post-mortem. The post-mortem report showed that he had died due to asphyxiation. As the body remained unidentified, rather than being burnt, it was buried in the Hindu burial ground of the Kodaikanal Municipality. In most cases, that would be where the story would end. The post-mortem report would be added to a thick stack of unclaimed body reports, and would make its way to a dusty corner of a government office and be quickly forgotten.

But not this time.

∽

In Velachery, a commercial and residential area in south Chennai not far from Kodaikanal, young Jeevajyothi was worried sick. Her husband, Prince Santhakumar, whom she had last seen on 26 October 2001, was taken away from her in very troubling circumstances. He had not contacted her for more than four days. With no information of his whereabouts or safety forthcoming, she was getting increasingly desperate.

She waited till 20 November 2001, losing hope with each passing day, before finally approaching the police. She then told them that she feared that he had been murdered.

. ❦

Being the daughter of an assistant manager of a popular chain of restaurants may not seem like the worst life to be living. But for a girl, being born in an orthodox family in India is a misfortune. The orthodox families would rather throw you under the bus than have you make your own life choices. This continues even after you become an adult. If your life choice involves falling in love and marrying someone the family does not approve of, then even the heavens might offer no solace.

Jeevajyothi hailed from one such orthodox family in Tamil Nadu. Her family had shifted to Chennai after selling off their properties in their native place, in search of a better life. First, it was her uncle who made the shift to Chennai. He got a job at the popular hotel chain, Saravana Bhavan. Soon, her father followed suit.

A job with this hotel chain was considered a dream. The owner of the restaurant chain, Pitchai Rajagopal, was fondly referred to as *Annachi* (elder brother) by his employees, who treated him like a demigod. And not without reason. A job in a restaurant by its very nature is considered 'temporary' owing to low wages, no paid time off and long shifts. However, Saravana Bhavan employees were an exception. They were well paid and enjoyed benefits like pension, free healthcare, housing loans, a marriage fund for their daughters and magazine subscriptions. These were benefits that would make even high-profile private-sector job holders envious.

If the restaurant chain did well, the employees did well too—salaries got better; the employees' children's education was taken care of; allowances improved; and even annual trips to their hometowns were included in the ever-growing list of perks. But employees who crossed the line by indulging in drinking (something Rajagopal frowned upon), or being engrossed in their mobile phones while on the job, were made to stand in line and disciplined after being summoned to his office.

Jeevajyothi's family was one among hundreds who stood to benefit from being Rajagopal's employees. After he joined, her uncle suggested that the family deposit ₹4.5 lakh with Rajagopal. He would keep the money, and hand out ₹6,000 or ₹7,000 every month to the family as 'interest' on the money that would be deposited with him. This was a 'scheme' to ensure that the family had a regular source of income, similar to the interest one can earn on a bank deposit.[2]

Pitchai Rajagopal had 'helped' Jeevajyothi's family in more than one way—he had agreed to employ both the brothers in his restaurant chain, and was supporting the family financially. It was something he thought he could take advantage of. His employees were exceptionally close and loyal to him. This gave him unparalleled clout in Tamil Nadu, so much so that he could literally have anyone in his pocket if he so wanted.

☙

Pitchai Rajagopal was born exactly 10 days before India

---

[2]Nath, Akshaya, 'Saravana Bhavan Murder: The Rise and Fall of Dosa King Rajagopal', *India Today*, 10 July 2019, https://tinyurl.com/47t46pap. Accessed on 12 July 2023.

formally earned its independence from the British—5 August 1947. He was born in Punnayadi, a village in Tuticorin district (now Thoothukudi), a coastal port city some 600 km south of Chennai. His father, Pitchai Nadar, was an onion seller; while his mother, Mani Ammal, was a housewife.

Rajagopal quit schooling after the seventh standard and moved to Chennai, where he began working as a busboy. Rajagopal's move to Chennai combined with his entrepreneurial spirit became the stepping stone for his future success. He set up a modest grocery store in Chennai's K.K. Nagar in 1968. At that time, the locality wasn't even considered part of the main city. Owing to his eye for business, he worked his way up to opening several grocery stores there by the late 1970s. As part of an expansion drive, he and his friend Ganapathi Iyer took over Kamatchi Bhavan (a nondescript restaurant) in a distress sale.

Rajagopal belonged to the Nadar caste, who are known to be a deeply devotional community. It is a popular belief among them that ventures bearing the name 'Saravana' (a variation of the names for Lord Murugan or Karthikeya, the elder son of Shiva and Parvati) rarely failed. When Rajagopal started his restaurant business, it was no surprise he named it Saravana.

Saravana Bhavan opened on 14 December 1981, serving what was already available in abundance in the city—South Indian vegetarian food. Restaurants like his were a-dime-a-dozen in every street of the city. But Saravana Bhavan had one difference. Legend has it that though a business advisor insisted that he use cheap ingredients and pay his staff little, Rajagopal actually did the opposite. He used coconut oil, good quality vegetables and paid his staff well.

At that time, he was selling all items at ₹1 per plate, despite knowing that he would be at a loss. But word spread about the tasty and cheap food being served at Saravana Bhavan and the rest, as they say, is history.

His restaurant earned a reputation and was soon referred to as the 'cultural icon' of Chennai. It became the go-to restaurant for the middle class in Chennai. An article in the *Hindustan Times* recounted, 'The show stopper was its sambar, a side dish that accompanied most items on its menu. Home cooks obsessed about recreating Saravana Bhavan's lentil and turmeric heavy version of the sambar.'[3]

According to *The New York Times*, Rajagopal struck upon the idea to open the restaurant 'when he overheard a salesman saying that he was planning to go to lunch in a town three miles away because there were no restaurants nearby.'[4]

As the tasty and inexpensive food gained a following among the price-conscious working class, his restaurant eventually turned a profit. He then used those to open more branches of his restaurant. Thus began his rise, and he later came to be known as the 'dosa king'.

As an article in the *Hindustan Times* analysed, the secret to Saravana Bhavan's success was the consistency in the taste of the food. Regardless of where you had their dosa and sambar, it tasted the same. The *getti* chutney was

---

[3]Vivek, T.R., 'The Man Who Built the Sarvana Bhavan Empire, and Murdered a Man, Has Died', *Hindustan Times*, 19 July 2019, https://bit.ly/3yn6aB5. Accessed on 9 March 2023.

[4]Tsang, Amie, 'P. Rajagopal, Restaurant Mogul Convicted of Murder, Dies at 71', *The New York Times*, 25 July 2019, https://nyti.ms/3ZcVqRz. Accessed on 2 March 2023.

a symbol of the high-quality ingredients they used, and the phrase even made it into pop culture.[5]

A column in *The News Minute*, written by Anjana Shekar, mentioned:

> Rajagopal entered into a business segment that had thus far been dominated by Brahmin cooks who considered 'vegetarian cooking' their area of expertise, at a time when people generally looked down upon the habit of eating out. Going out for lunch or dinner was not an idea easily digested back then. And Rajagopal, who was from the Nadar community, positioned himself with poise and confidence, catering exclusively to the middle-class south Indian vegetarian diners.[6]

For many years the chain comprised seven outlets in Chennai, usually in hubs where a meal during lunch hours would be much sought after. In 2000, after having opened in about 20 locations in India, Saravana Bhavan ventured overseas. The chain expanded first into Dubai, then to cities like New York, London and Sydney. From Canada to Singapore, it served tasty food to homesick South Indians. They opened in neighbourhoods where the Indian diaspora had a strong presence. Over the years, the chain grew to 80 outlets overseas and to about 30 in India. It became one

---

[5]Vivek, T.R., 'The Man Who Built the Sarvana Bhavan Empire, and Murdered a Man, Has Died', *Hindustan Times*, 19 July 2019, https://bit.ly/3yn6aB5. Accessed on 9 March 2023.

[6]Shekar, Anjana, 'The Rise and Fall of Saravana Bhavan Rajagopal: The "Dosa King" with a Notorious Past', *The News Minute*, 18 July 2019, https://bit.ly/3J5HYJv. Accessed on 2 March 2023.

of India's biggest restaurant chains, with annual revenues close to ₹3,000 crore.[7]

But Rajagopal had a fault. He was a deeply superstitious man. As he revealed in his autobiography, *Vetri Meedhu Aasai Veithen* (*I Set my Heart on Victory*), he started his restaurants based on the advice of his astrologer. The astrologer had told him that if he wanted to get rich, he should enter a business which involved 'fire'. He took the advice seriously and started the restaurant. With this advice having paid off handsomely, Rajagopal wasn't about to start doubting his astrologer. So, when the astrologer advised him to marry the daughter of one of his employees, he took that to be the will of God.

∞

Jeevajyothi was still a child then, residing with her family in a colony taken on lease by Hotel Saravana Bhavan for its employees. The family sought the help of a home tutor, Prince Santhakumar, to help her younger brother ace his maths class. And Jeevajyothi, who was still in her teens then, took a liking to the tutor.

In her conservative family, where caste was writ large, it was already a task for the free-spirited youth to do their will. It was even more difficult if you were a woman. For Jeevajyothi, this meant that her love for Santhakumar was forbidden. He was a Christian and that too from a different caste, and her father Ramaswamy did not consent to the relationship.

---

[7]Fernandes, Jocelyn, 'The Downfall of Dosa Kingpin and Saravana Bhavan Founder P Rajagopal', *moneycontrol*, 18 July 2019, https://tinyurl.com/2yrp9pnr. Accessed on 27 July 2023.

In most situations, this would be a family's 'internal' problem. The embarrassed parents would try and keep the affair hidden for as long as they could, hoping the phase would pass. But the matter did not remain internal in this case, and Rajagopal got involved.

Unknown to the family, Rajagopal had taken a 'fancy' for his assistant manager's daughter. He was already married, not once but twice. In 1972, he married his first wife who bore him two sons. Subsequently, he 'took away' the wife of one of his employees as his second wife in 1994. But being the adored annachi, who had squads of employees more than eager to do his bidding, Rajagopal got away with it. Now, Rajagopal 'decided' he wanted to take Jeevajyothi as his third 'simultaneous' wife. Whether this was because he was advised by an astrologer to grow his business and prosperity, or whether it was because he had a liking for Jeevajyothi, remains unknown. Being the rich and powerful man that he was, he was used to having his way. This time too, he thought that it would be no different. It was to be a fairly simple case of bulldozing his way into the heart of a meek and unresisting young girl, too intimidated and lacking in social and family support.

Rajagopal began his plan by trying to ensure that the love between Jeevajyothi and Santhakumar didn't blossom. He made it known that he didn't 'like' that Santhakumar was visiting the family home to tutor her brother. As the family was staying in accommodation provided by the company, Rajagopal issued the ultimatum that either Santhakumar should stop visiting the house or that they should vacate the accommodation.

Rather than cowering, the family decided to shift out

and found a new place for themselves in the MGR Nagar area of Chennai. This was also possible because Jeevajyothi's father decided to look for greener pastures abroad. He resigned from his job and left for Malaysia.

For a while, things seemed calm. But Jeevajyothi was madly in love with Santhakumar, and wasn't about to give up on him easily. As the months passed, Santhakumar got a job as a career agent at the Life Insurance Corporation (LIC). With some form of financial stability attained, the couple decided that they would get married.

Rather than trying to convince her family to accept her choice, Jeevajyothi eloped. They were married in the office of the sub registrar (Anna Nagar) on 28 April 1999. The couple then left for Madurai, a city towards the hills of Tamil Nadu more than 400 km away from Chennai. It was only from afar that she contacted her mother to inform that she had got married.

Her mother brought them back to Chennai and arranged for a ceremony in a temple in Thiruvanmiyur. Jeevajyothi and her husband started living in a house at Kottivakkam locality.

A few months into the marriage, Jeevajyothi began to work at a travel agency at Thiruvanmiyur. She worked there for three years, while her husband continued to work at the LIC.

But soon, her ambition grew. The couple decided that they would start their own travel agency. They initially turned to Jeevajyothi's family for help. Her uncle pitched in and helped start 'Global Air Travels'. They opened an office at Velachery in Chennai. As she needed more money, Jeevajyothi approached her mother. Her mother, in turn, reached out to Rajagopal for help. This was the first in a series of big mistakes.

For a while, Rajagopal said he didn't want to help. Eventually, he agreed to hand over the money. However, he had a condition—the couple would have to visit Mani Mandapam (a shrine) he had built at Vellore, so that they could offer prayers. He would then hand over the cash at that place. Since they obliged, he too kept his word and handed out a 'loan' of ₹1 lakh to help the business find its footing.

After the loan, he began making his intentions known more aggressively. Under the pretext of financially helping the family, he started trying to woo Jeevajyothi by gifting her expensive jewellery and other gifts. He even tried to sow doubts in her mind about her husband. He now had a pretext to frequently contact Jeevajyothi. He used to call her every day, either while she was at work or even when she was at home. He also reached out to the family inquiring about their well-being, and tried to be a godfather to them. He would hang around at the family shop and engage with her family for a long time.

∽

In September 2001, on account of an ailment, Jeevajyothi was admitted to Malar hospital. As soon as he heard the news, Rajagopal visited the hospital with his 'pals' like a typical mafia boss. He 'declared' that Jeevajyothi was not being given adequate treatment, and that she should be shifted to another hospital where a doctor of their choice (Dr Lalitha) was posted. Jeevajyothi, it seemed, didn't have a choice regarding where she should be treated. She was not consulted about whether she was happy with the treatment being offered either. While she was hospitalized, Rajagopal handed Jeevajyothi a mobile phone (still a luxury at that time).

As directed by Rajagopal, Jeevajyothi was discharged from Malar Hospital and admitted to Vijaya Nursing Home. There, she was asked to undergo certain tests. Subsequently, she was told that the problem was not with her and rather it was her husband who needed to be tested.

Bemused, her husband wondered why he had to be tested. He was also told that they should not have intercourse prior to the test. The night she was discharged, Rajagopal phoned her close to midnight to remind her about 'Dr Lalitha's advice' that the couple should not have intercourse prior to Santhakumar's tests. From the hospital, Santhakumar telephoned Jeevajyothi that he was being asked to undergo HIV and other tests. He immediately refused to take the test.

A few days after she resumed work, Rajagopal called her again. He said, 'Your husband has refused to undergo an HIV test. I already knew that he would refuse.' Rajagopal was trying to convince Jeevajyothi that her husband might be HIV positive. He even went on to say that Santhakumar refused to take the test to conceal this fact. This was a somewhat infantile ploy to try and get her to abandon her husband. Rajagopal was on a mission to not just separate Jeevajyothi from her husband, but to also make it seem that he only had her best interests in mind.

Unsuccessful in his plans so far, Rajagopal decided that he had to take things up a notch. On 28 September 2001, at about 12.30 a.m., Rajagopal, along with Jeevajyothi's parents, barged into her house. They started berating her for her 'irresponsible attitude.'

However, rather than getting intimidated, Jeevajyothi decided that she would give it back to them. She threatened Rajagopal that she would complain about his behaviour to the police. It was not a difficult task for her. She was a young girl who had already broken centuries of family tradition and married outside what her family considered acceptable. Now she was simply taking on the local behemoth.

Rajagopal reacted in a typical fashion. He thrust his cellphone towards her and dared her to call the police. He warned her that no matter which police she approached, he would handle them. As the High Court later mentioned in the hearing, he also quite unabashedly told her that Kiruthiga, his second wife, had also initially resisted him and had even got protection for herself. However, now that she had relented and agreed to marry him, she was living a 'queen's life'.

He looked Santhakumar in the eye and told him that he wanted Jeevajyothi as his third wife. He threatened him to separate from her in two days or face the consequences. Three days later, on 1 October 2001, Rajagopal called Santhakumar and quite plainly asked him whether he had made up his mind to leave Jeevajyothi. He also pointed out that more than two days had lapsed since he was given an ultimatum to separate from her.

Not knowing what to do, Jeevajyothi and Santhakumar decided to leave town without informing anyone. However, when they tried to leave, Rajagopal's henchmen were waiting outside their house. Even her family was there outside.

The couple was accosted and, along with her family members, were made to sit in an Ambassador car and driven to Chandrasekar's house (Rajagopal's friend) at K.K. Nagar.

This place was used as a godown for Saravana Bhavan. It was sometimes also used as Rajagopal's lair. After they reached there, Rajagopal also arrived. Without saying a word, he folded his dhoti and began beating Santhakumar to a pulp with his bare hands. His henchmen also joined in. Jeevajyothi pleaded for her husband's life with folded hands.

Santhakumar tried to take his wife and leave from there. He was threatened that if he ever touched his wife again, he would be beaten even more. Rajagopal then directed his henchmen to take Santhakumar away and thrash him. Jeevajyothi was left weeping in a corner of the room.

A thundering Rajagopal then told Jeevajyothi that he could do whatever he wanted to her but was choosing not to stoop to that level. This was a not-so-subtle threat that he could rape her if he wanted. He would 'prefer' that she first agree to marry him and become his third wife.

The next day, one of Rajagopal's foremost henchmen (Daniel) called Jeevajyothi and expressed his regret for the previous day's happenings. He suggested that she should lodge a complaint against Rajagopal before the commissioner of police.

On 13 October 2001, Jeevajyothi and Santhakumar went to the city police commissioner and lodged a complaint informing the police about the assault. They were not aware that they were being surveilled by Rajagopal's men. When they returned home, they noticed from a distance that their house had been surrounded by Rajagopal's men.

Daniel advised them to stay in a lodge at Egmore. He even began helping them with what they should do next. He informed them that Jeevajyothi's father had lodged a 'missing' complaint with the police. He also gave them other information to help avoid Rajagopal. But could Daniel be trusted?

Daniel promised to help the couple reach out to the media. He then asked Santhakumar to meet with a press reporter that he personally knew. He asked Santhakumar to come alone. They were to meet near a Sai Baba Temple. However, rather than sending him alone, Jeevajyothi decided to go along with Santhakumar. And her fears turned out to be right. Things were about to go from bad to worse.

∞

On 18 October 2001, Jeevajyothi and Santhakumar arrived in the vicinity of the Sai Baba Temple around 6.00 p.m. Two Ambassador cars and a Tata Sumo came and halted behind their car. Two of the henchmen, armed with knives, alighted from the first car. Jeevajyothi and Santhakumar were forcibly made to board the first car, and driven to an unknown spot. There they stopped for about 10 minutes.

As noted in the court judgment, the car then started again and stopped at Chengalpattu for about 30 minutes. There, another Tata Sumo came and stopped in front of their car. At about 8.30 p.m., a Mercedes Benz that belonged to Rajagopal arrived there. Jeevajyothi's mother alighted from the Benz and told her that Rajagopal (seated in the Benz) was calling her to meet him.

When Jeevajyothi resisted, she was forcibly taken by two men. Inside the car, she saw her father seated along with Rajagopal. As they were driving, Rajagopal pulled out a file and tauntingly showed Jeevajyothi a copy of the police complaint she had filed against him. He then teased her about the fate of her complaint. All Jeevajyothi could do was beg to be allowed to join her husband. All she was told was that she would meet her husband at Trichy, where the convoy of cars was headed.

The following day Jeevajyothi was taken to Parappadi village to meet a priest, who performed 'black magic'. He was instructed to 'cure' her of whatever spell she was under. From there, she was taken to another village named Veppankulam to seek *kuri* (a fortune teller's advice). The fortune teller there told her that her husband had escaped, and his whereabouts were not known.

Jeevajyothi's and her family spent the night at a hotel in Tirunelveli, and thereafter they left for Chennai by train. Jeevajyothi was worried sick about her husband's fate. It came as a huge relief to her when he called her on 21 October 2001. She was relieved that he was still alive, but the news that he had to share was grim.

Santhakumar told Jeevajyothi that he had been in Daniel's custody. Apparently, Daniel told Santhakumar that he was offered ₹5 lakh to 'finish him off' but that he had taken pity on him. Out of sympathy, Daniel had let him go unharmed. However, there was a condition. It was that he would leave town and head to Bombay (now Mumbai). Santhakumar asked Jeevajyothi to join him in Bombay, after escaping in whatever way she could.

However, Jeevajyothi told him that it was next to impossible for her to escape as she was under watch all the time. Her every move was being tracked. Instead, she suggested that he should come to her parents' house (where she was being held), so that they could both plead with Rajagopal to pardon them and let them go. Santhakumar agreed. He came to Jeevajyothi's house and accordingly sought a meeting with Rajagopal. Predictably, this turned out to be a huge mistake.

Rajagopal promptly came over and the couple pleaded for mercy. They assured him that they would withdraw the police complaint filed against him. Jeevajyothi, along with Santhakumar, her parents and her brother were all taken to the Vadapalani Office building by Rajagopal's men.

The family were kept in a waiting room while Rajagopal summoned Daniel and asked him how on earth Santhakumar was still alive. Daniel had gone on to narrate graphic details of the manner in which he had 'murdered' Santhakumar. The court document later noted that, given his penchant for theatrics, Rajagopal asked Daniel whether the man standing before them was a brother of Santhakumar or his ghost who had come back from the dead.

After being disgraced in front of his boss, Daniel assaulted Santhakumar for his 'betrayal.' The other henchmen too joined in the beating. Jeevajyothi and her father both went to 'rescue' Santhakumar. She was pushed away and her father was also thrashed for intervening.

On 24 October 2001, Jeevajyothi and her husband were taken to the Guindy commissioner of police and then to Metropolitan Magistrate Court for withdrawal of the police complaint. As dictated by Yaanai Rajendran, an advocate who was present there, Jeevajyothi wrote and signed a letter to the police purporting to withdraw the police complaint. She also had to agree that she had lodged it while she was under duress. Her signatures and that of her husband, parents and brother were also obtained on blank papers.

On 26 October 2001, at about 6.30 a.m., one of the henchmen came to them and declared that Rajagopal had called for Santhakumar. Unwilling to send him alone, Jeevajyothi also went along with him. Rajagopal was waiting at the lobby by the side of a Tata Sumo and asked them to get into the car, saying that he wanted to discuss an important matter with them.

They set off and another Tata Sumo followed them. After a journey of about 10–12 minutes, the first car stopped near Karai Iruppu. The other Tata Sumo also stopped, and the men from the second car joined them. Rajagopal dragged Santhakumar out of the car and handed him over to the men. He directed them to finish him off.

The men took him and drove off in the direction of Dindigul. That was the last Jeevajyothi saw of her husband. Despite her protests, she was pushed angrily inside the vehicle by Rajagopal. He came back to the car and they drove back. Upon returning, Rajagopal asked her family to 'discuss' with her all that needed to be done.

Even after all of this, Jeevajyothi was being surveilled by Rajagopal's men. They remained there from 26 October till 6 November 2001 but she received no information regarding her husband.

On 28 October 2001, one fortune teller was sent to tell her that her husband was wandering as a deranged person and may return after three years. On 6 November 2001, they went to their native place. Jeevajyothi waited hopefully till 20 November and then finally approached the police. By this time, word began to get out that Rajagopal had carried out his threat. The police could no longer ignore the case.

Perhaps, on account of the public pressure, this time

the police took the case up in earnest. Rajagopal thought it would be best to surrender and upon being interrogated, confessed to committing Santhakumar's murder.

Daniel was also arrested and confessed that he and the other accused had killed Santhakumar and thrown the body in the TigerChola forest area near a curve on the road. Thanks to his revelations, the investigation team eventually determined that the body found by the forest officials on 31 October 2001 was that of Santhakumar.

∞

During the trial, Jeevajyothi was residing at Thethakudi village in Nagapattinam district along with her parents. Within a few months of his arrest, Rajagopal was granted bail. Rather than abiding by the bail conditions, on 15 July 2003, Rajagopal, his legal adviser (Rajendran) and his men went to Thethakudi village with ₹6 lakh in cash. They went to Jeevajyothi and asked her not to give evidence in the murder case as well as in the abduction case and compelled her to receive the cash. Rajendran also asked her to give evidence in favour of the defence. When she refused and screamed at them for even attempting to bribe her, her brother Ramkumar and other relatives intervened.

Rajagopal then asked his henchmen to attack her and her brother. One of the accused attacked Ramkumar with a knife, hurting his right hand. In the meantime, the villagers gathered there on hearing the hue and cry. Rajagopal swiftly left the spot. Unfortunately, for him, Rajendran was not able to get into the escape car and was caught red-handed by the villagers. They then handed him over to the police after thrashing him. Rajagopal's bail was cancelled.

With the police building a watertight case against him, and his attempts to bribe witnesses largely failing, Rajagopal felt the net closing.

In 2004, the trial court found Rajagopal and Daniel guilty of culpable homicide and sentenced them to 10 years in prison. Rajagopal appealed to the Madras High Court. But the move backfired. Rather than the rule going in his favour, the High Court enhanced his conviction to murder and instead of 10 years, he was sentenced to life imprisonment.

Rajagopal was not a man to give up. He challenged the sentence in the Supreme Court, but it did not work for him. In March 2019, the Supreme Court upheld the High Court's verdict. It gave him 100 days' time to surrender and begin his jail term.

Citing health reasons, Rajapoal refused to surrender and instead sought more time from the court. But there was no leniency shown to him. The Supreme Court rejected his petition and told him to surrender. Rajagopal died of cardiac arrest at a Chennai hospital barely a week after he surrendered.

∽

Did Rajagopal ever regret his relentless pursuit of Jeevajyothi and the murder of Santhakumar? In an interview with *The New York Times*, Rajagopal denied having anything to do with it. He said, 'I used to pray to my god, why was I punished for someone else's mistake?'[8] However, he did give a hint that he didn't 'like' that he went after Jeevajyothi.

---

[8]Romig, Rollo, 'Masala Dosa to Die for', *The New York Times Magazine*, 7 May 2014, https://nyti.ms/40dYCgf. Accessed on 24 March 2023.

Jeevajyothi never came to terms with the fact that the man who ruined her life got away without serving his sentence. In a report, she said: 'At that young age it proved a huge loss to me. […] Now, even though I feel sorry for his death the fact that he died without spending a single day in prison will not allow my husband's soul to rest in peace. To me, it will remain an irremediable wound.'[9]

Jeevajyothi revealed the hell she had to go through on account of her willingness to take on the mighty. The lurid details of the case printed by Tamil weekly magazines reeked of speculation and gossip, not so subtly hinting that Jeevajyothi too could have been partly 'responsible' for 'luring' Rajagopal into his pursuit.

Rajagopal's pursuit of Jeevajyothi, despite her disinterest, proved a killer blow for one of India's most successful food brands. An article in the *Hindustan Times* said, 'Its headquarters in Chennai's Vadapalani, also one of its largest restaurants by size, now resembles a warehouse in disuse. The eatery itself is a shadow of its former self with the colour on display pictures fading away.'[10]

---

[9]Emmanuel, Gladwin, 'Jeevajothi Unable to Accept That P Rajagopal Died without Spending a Single Day in Prison', *Mumbai Mirror*, 19 July 2019, https://bit.ly/3LQPJVp. Accessed on 24 March 2023.

[10]Vivek, T.R., 'The Man Who Built the Sarvana Bhavan Empire, and Murdered a Man, Has Died', *Hindustan Times*, 19 July 2019, https://bit.ly/3yn6aB5. Accessed on 9 March 2023.

7

THE HAND THAT ROCKS THE CRADLE

The murder of investigative journalist
Shivani Bhatnagar[1]

Death is not bound to follow [a] beaten track. It is known for wending its ways weirdly. On 23.01.99, Shivani Bhatnagar, a young journalist was at her home... [in] Delhi, rejoicing [in the] company of [an] infant born of her loins about three months back. Death approached her in disguise, having sweets in hands but snare incognito. She was found like a sitting duck. There was none in the house along with [the] deceased except that baby who knew nothing except to smile.

Additional Sessions Judge Rajendra Kumar Shastri couldn't have said it better when describing the murder of *The Indian Express* journalist, Shivani Bhatnagar. She was found dead in her home in East Delhi in early 1999.

For three years after the murder, this was a blind case.

---

[1]Quotations and case details from: State v. (I) Ravi Kant Sharma s/o Sh. J.D., S.C. no. 14/06, FIR No. 21/99, Karkardooma Courts, Delhi, 18 March 2008.

The usual suspects, including her husband, were rounded up and questioned. Her recent activities were scrutinized, and her friends and acquaintances were examined. But the police were not any wiser—no one knew who killed Shivani or why.

And then, seemingly out of the blue, three years later, the police claimed to have found the culprits. This threw the case right into the spotlight. It was covered by news channels with breathless haste and was even discussed in Parliament, where the opposition parties gunned for the ruling party. They threatened to drag Pramod Mahajan, the blue-eyed boy of the then ruling BJP (Bharatiya Janata Party) government, through the mud. Shivani was killed for having loved—for having loved and lost.

ॐ

On the morning of 23 January 1999, unknown to the Bhatnagars, two people with the same name, Ved Prakash—although one went by an alias Kalu—lurked outside their building. They kept a watch on the goings-on around the Navkunj Apartments (Pratapganj, New Delhi). Within the building, life was normal—a servant preparing breakfast; men leaving the home for the day's work; and Shivani busying herself with the chores of motherhood, having given birth just three months back. Nothing seemed amiss within Flat B-42.

Shivani's husband's brother-in-law, B.S. Bhatnagar (who lived in Panchkula), had spent the previous night at their place. He left the house at around 10.00 a.m. for a scheduled meeting after having breakfast. Her husband, Rakesh Bhatnagar, too left for work at around 12.15 p.m., leaving Shivani at home with her son Tanmay and servant Vally. During the lunch hour, Vally also left the house.

At around 3.00 p.m., Shivani called her husband to tell him that one Mr Sharma had come over to hand over a wedding card on behalf of a person named Adhikari. This Adhikari allegedly worked at *The Tribune* in Chandigarh, and his son was to be married. Rakesh even spoke to this Mr Sharma, after his wife handed over the phone to him. That was the last time Rakesh spoke to Shivani.

B.S. Bhatnagar returned to the flat at around 5.00 p.m. and tried to open it with the duplicate key that Rakesh had given him. However, since the key didn't seem to work, he called Rakesh to ask for a solution. Rakesh asked him to turn the keys twice on the fulcrum, with a bit of jiggling to get it to turn. Twenty minutes later, Rakesh received a call from his brother-in-law again. He still could not get the door to open. After another 15–20 minutes, Rakesh received yet another call. Rakesh thought that it was again about the door, but this time his brother-in-law was panicking. 'Shivani was stabbed and is lying motionless on the floor!' B.S. Bhatnagar screamed.

All hell broke loose at *The Times of India* office, where Rakesh worked as the legal editor. Rakesh broke down and rushed out of the office, heading straight home. A colleague informed the police, and urgently asked them to head to their address. Rakesh reached his house and found Shivani lying motionless in front of their bedroom. She was taken to the nearby SDN Hospital. Chief Medical Officer Dr Piyush Jain declared her 'brought dead'. Refusing to break down, unwilling to accept the doctor's verdict and holding on to hope, Rakesh carried her to Apollo Hospital. However, it was not to be—Shivani had breathed her last.

But Rakesh's ordeal was just beginning. The complaint

he filed, as recorded in the court document, described the sequence of events and ended with a graphic description. It noted:

> At about 5.30 pm, I again received a phone call from Sh. B.S Bhatnagar who beseeched me to come soon as Shivani was stabbed. I reached my house at about 6.00 PM and found Shivani lying injured in the bedroom. There was bleeding from her neck. One kitchen knife was stuck in her neck and another similar knife was lying on her abdomen. One griddle (tawa) and a piece of electric wire (yellow color) [were] lying near her body. Household articles from all three bedrooms and almirahs were scattered here and there. Two cups full of tea and snacks in a plate were lying near the sofa in the drawing room. Two empty glass tumblers were seen on the dining table and one sweet box was kept near the sofa. I called the police immediately.

Rakesh's complaint was brief but offered no indication as to who might be behind this. Instead, owing to rumours of a deteriorating relationship with his wife, he emerged as a prime suspect. Despite being interrogated by the police for long hours and also being subjected to a polygraph test, his examiners observed 'no deception' in his responses.

With the police completely in the dark, the investigation had hit a dead end. At this point, all the police were able to establish was that it was a friendly entry rather than a forced one. The assailants had ransacked the flat to make the murder look like part of a robbery attempt. They later admitted that this was done in a bid to throw the police off their scent.

The investigating officer for the case was changed four times. On 24 January 1999, the investigation was transferred to the Crime Branch Inspector Sukhwinder Singh. He was in charge until 26 April 2000, when it was handed over to Inspector Ranbir Singh. He handed over the investigation to Inspector Ran Singh after some time. It was when Inspector Inder Singh took over the investigation on 18 June 2002 that things finally began to change.

Inder Singh was the investigating officer of another murder case, when he received a tip-off that one Pradeep Sharma could give some clues about Shivani Bhatnagar's murder case. What had been a blind case until now suddenly began to see a flicker of light—nearly three years later.

When Inspector Pawan Sharma (working under Inder Singh) received the tip-off, the police took quick action. It wasn't long before a man named Sri Bhagwan was arrested. He was the first to name IPS (Indian Police Service) R.K. Sharma in connection with the case. R.K. Sharma was a senior police officer that Bhagwan knew well. Bhagwan's father Onkar Sharma, a police officer, had served under R.K. Sharma. Their equation went beyond work, and the two were good friends.

Bhagwan was first called into questioning before an investigating officer on 23 July 2002. However, since he was avoiding questions and not much could be extracted from him, he was allowed to go home. But his freedom did not last long. He was arrested seven days later on 30 July 2002, and was subjected to custodial interrogation. He was interrogated about the calls he had made and received via his phone. It was only at that point that he revealed that the calls were made to R.K. Sharma. The call records testified that Sri Bhagwan and R.K. Sharma spoke frequently with each other between 4 and 11 January 1999, a little more than 10 days before Shivani was found dead. Bhagwan was soon singing like a canary, and even took the police to show the STD booths from which the calls were made on the day of the incident. His disclosures soon pointed to the role of R.K. Sharma in the crime.

With Bhagwan's disclosures, the police were able to draw up a coherent story into what went down in the killing of Shivani Bhatnagar.

⌀

Shivani Bhatnagar wasn't just any journalist. She was a star reporter at *The Indian Express*. The set of 'beats' that she used to cover included the investigating agencies like the Central Bureau of Investigation (CBI), Intelligence Bureau (IB) and the biggest of them all—the Prime Minister's Office (PMO).

These were the days before WhatsApp and encrypted chats. Shivani joined *The Indian Express* as a principal correspondent in Delhi in 1997. At that time, any journalist needed to cultivate sources by meeting officers; spending time with important people (including ministers); and by building a relationship of trust with them. This was the only way a source would be considered reliable. The journalists with the best access were (and continue to be) prized by newspaper editorial teams for their ability to deliver information, exclusive stories and they have insider knowledge of the workings of the highest levels of government. Journalists built relationships with important decision-makers and with those familiar with crucial information within the government.

These relationships were kept strictly professional, lest a conflict of interest might arise.

However, the lines between the journalist and their source would sometimes blur. Favours would be sought and exchanged, as the journalists were eager to keep the sources happy. The sources were also eager not to rub the journalists the wrong way, lest they decide to run an exposé on the source (especially if it was something incriminating).

Shivani had honed the art of treading the fine line between a personal and professional relationship with her sources—at least with most of them. In some cases, things got out of hand. It was through her rounds of the PMO as part of her job 'to glean tidbits'—as the trial court judge later described—that Shivani met R.K. Sharma. The suave and polished IPS officer was posted at the PMO as an Officer on Special Duty (OSD) between 1997 and 1998.

❦

R.K. Sharma began his career with the Haryana Police. By the 1980s, he was posted as Gurgaon's (now Gurugram) superintendent of police. At that time, Gurgaon was just arid farmland and did not have the swanky and gaudy high-rises dotting the dusty skyline. It was around this time that R.K. Sharma got his first deputation to the CBI. This was a stint that helped him climb the career ladder in a way other cops at his designation could only dream about. A few years later, he was in Lyons (France) for a three-year spell at the Interpol headquarters. It is perhaps there that R.K. Sharma polished his French, and earned a taste for exquisite French wines and cheese that later charmed Shivani.

In July 1995, R.K. Sharma returned to work with the

Haryana Police once again. The personnel rules stipulated that he would have to spend the next three years there. But his luck was about to change. At a time when Indian politics was in a state of flux, I.K. Gujral became the prime minister (PM) in the United Front government backed by the Congress.

R.K. Sharma was no ordinary officer. He was at a high position because of influence—thanks to the family he hailed from as well as the family he married into. His father J.D. Sharma was an IAS (Indian Administrative Service) officer. Even more influential was R.K. Sharma's wife Madhu's family. Madhu's father, S.V. Bedi, was a senior editor at *The Tribune* (an influential Chandigarh-based newspaper). Raj Bedi, Madhu's mother, was also a noted stage personality. It was through the Bedis that R.K. Sharma came to connect with I.K. Gujral.

Owing to the connections between I.K. Gujral and R.K. Sharma, the latter was quickly granted a plum post. It was under him that R.K. Sharma worked as an OSD. An article in *India Today* magazine, which covered the developments of Shivani's case, mentioned that since there was no PMO vacancy at the level of director, Sharma was appointed as the PM's personal staff. The article claimed: 'The PMO was in such a tearing hurry that it didn't even inform the Home Ministry— the controlling authority for IPS officers' appointment—but sent a direct wireless message to the Haryana government on June 24 1997, asking it to relieve Sharma.'[2]

༄

---

[2]Vinayak, Ramesh, 'Shivani Bhatnagar Murder: Suspect No. 1 IPS officer R.K. Sharma was Politically Well Connected', *India Today*, 2 September 2002, https://bit.ly/3LNB6SU. Accessed on 24 March 2023.

Shivani was introduced to R.K. Sharma in 1997 by an aide of a Congress Member of Parliament (MP) while she was purportedly chasing a story. This story was about a medical college, supposedly promoted by the family of Bahujan Samaj Party (BSP) politician Mayawati. Over the course of the following year, Shivani and R.K. Sharma grew close. The relationship went from being a formal source–journalist relationship, to a casual first-name basis relationship. They then proceeded to meet outside formal settings for late-night dinners and parties.

R.K. Sharma later allegedly confessed to the police the nature of his relationship with Shivani:

> Reporter Shivani Bhatnagar was a frequent visitor to PMO in connection with her work...and we frequently used to interact... I visited her several times in the absence of her husband, from December 1997 to March 1998. We called each other on phone to fix meetings which were generally at her house and Santusthi, and sometimes in Connaught Place. We spent some good time together due to which I developed intimacy with her.[3]

However, since confessions to the police can be extracted using 'extrajudicial means', these could not be used as evidence in court or held against the accused. Hence, it should be read keeping in mind the usual disclaimers.

Sensitive documents purportedly sourced from R.K. Sharma were found in Shivani's flat after her murder. The police later used this to try and prove a close relationship

---

[3]"I Was Desperate to Get Rid of Shivani"', *The Times of India*, 20 March 2008, https://bit.ly/3FIWZPp. Accessed on 24 March 2023.

between the two. According to the police, R.K. Sharma had provided three secret documents from the PMO to Shivani. She wanted to publish some sensational article based on them. This, the prosecution said, was proof of the cozy relationship between the two. The prosecution said that the duo took their relationship beyond just professional matters and working hours of the day.

R.K. Sharma was 15 years senior to Shivani, but that seemed to have no bearing on what soon blossomed into a full-blown affair. Perhaps, his worldliness left Shivani impressed; or maybe the quid pro quo kept taking them deeper and deeper into their newfound relationship. Allegedly, the relationship had even hit a point where they promised to divorce their respective partners. Such was the nature of their relationship that even her email password was reportedly 'Ravikant'.

However, the bliss didn't last forever. Shivani travelled to London for three months between March and June 1998 on a scholarship. During her stay in London, she confided in Sejal Shah (her roommate) that she was deeply in love with R.K. Sharma. She even revealed that she was pregnant and that they were planning to build a life together.

Sejal later testified about the happenings in London. As per her testimony, Shivani and R.K. Sharma had developed an instant liking for each other. They were sharing an intimate relationship. Sejal explained that Shivani used to receive phone calls from R.K. Sharma every day. She knew this as she used to pick up the phone at times.[4]

---

[4]Ravi Kant Sharma v. State, CRL.A. 357/2008, Delhi High Court, 12 November 2011.

However, mid-way through Shivani's stay in London, things took a turn for the worse. Sejal recalled Shivani being very upset as R.K. Sharma had started ignoring her. She used to cry a lot. Sejal also recalled that Shivani had confided in her that R.K. Sharma was 'scared' of his wife. It soon became apparent that R.K. Sharma was stalling on the promises of abandoning his family in favour of Shivani.

Shivani returned to India in June 1998 and gave birth to a baby boy in October, at the Jessa Ram hospital in Karol Bagh (Delhi). It was after the delivery that things took an ugly turn. Shivani's sister, Sewanti, accompanied her to the hospital during the time of her delivery. Sewanti later told the court that Shivani asked her to call R.K. Sharma and inform him about the birth of her child. Shivani even told her to inform him that she needed an electronic bottle sterilizer. She wanted him to bring it to her.

Sewanti told the court that she called R.K. Sharma three times but could not contact him. She then called him again the following day and conveyed the message. She told the court that Shivani was taken aback to find that R.K. Sharma reacted indifferently to the news. Sewanti also noticed that Shivani then became depressed and upset.

By this time, I.K. Gujral was no longer the PM. Before leaving the position, he granted his loyal officer one last favour. Despite objections from the Department of Personnel, owing to his lack of experience and lack of a 'consistently outstanding record'[5], R.K. Sharma was transferred to Mumbai

---

[5]Vinayak, Ramesh, 'Shivani Bhatnagar Murder: Suspect No. 1 IPS officer R.K. Sharma was Politically Well Connected', *India Today*, 2 September 2002, https://bit.ly/3LNB6SU. Accessed on 24 March 2023.

as the chief vigilance officer of Air India. Allegedly, this file was signed on Gujral's last day as the PM.

R.K. Sharma allegedly told the cops in a confessional statement that all was going smoothly till the middle of September 1998. Since he had shifted to Mumbai, he wasn't able to visit Delhi frequently and even started avoiding Shivani's calls. She did not like this, and blackmailed him based on some documents she had in her possession. He said that by the time Sewanti informed him about the child, he had lost interest in Shivani.[6]

The prosecution connected the dots where some would argue none existed. Referring to the call details, the prosecution pointed out that between December 1997 and May 1998, there were about 68 calls between Shivani and R.K. Sharma. They said that this clearly suggested that R.K. Sharma and Shivani Bhatnagar were known to each other, and were talking regularly. This was contradictory to R.K. Sharma's defence. He had said that he only had a professional relationship with Shivani and knew her as a family friend. Even when Shivani went to London, the calls between her and R.K. Sharma continued. It was after the birth of her son that the number of calls between the two declined significantly.

Armed with this information, the prosecution built a case that Shivani wanted to marry R.K. Sharma after divorcing their respective spouses. However, the apathy he showed upon the birth of their child must have hurt Shivani. She must have then threatened to expose his 'misdeeds'

---

[6]"I was Desperate to Get Rid of Shivani'", *The Times of India*, 20 March 2008, https://bit.ly/3FIWZPp. Accessed on 24 March 2023.

in revenge. She allegedly vowed to 'ruin him', by exposing the amorous letters he had written to her. She threatened to send those to his wife, along with making them public.

The police said that anticipating the damage Shivani could do to his career and reputation, R.K. Sharma must have decided to eliminate her. To carry out his plan, he must have dipped into his old contacts, who could get him a 'toughie' to carry out the job. R.K. Sharma denied any wrongdoing. The onus was on the police to stitch together a string of seemingly unconnected events, and ascertain R.K. Sharma's role in the case.

On 12 January 1999, R.K. Sharma—who was by then posted in Mumbai—paid a visit to Delhi. It was said that he was there to meet the then joint secretary and the chief vigilance commissioner in the Ministry of Civil Aviation. According to the police, no such meeting actually took place. Instead, R.K. Sharma (who was staying at Ashoka Hotel) met with Bhagwan on 13 January 1999. Bhagwan brought with him three others—Satya Prakash, Ved Prakash Sharma and Ved Prakash (Kalu)—to plan the hit job. The police claimed that these five men conspired to eliminate Shivani. He even invited Shivani to the hotel, so that the others could see her. R.K. Sharma later allegedly confessed to the police saying: 'Thereafter, I asked the men to eliminate her.'[7] He then took them to show Navkunj Apartments.

R.K. Sharma also allegedly said, 'We reached the apartments and parked the vehicle outside the flat. I pointed

---

[7]Ibid.

towards the location of Shivani's flat and went inside. I spoke to her for about half-an-hour and then returned to the car.' He further added, 'I had told them not to worry about the subsequent police investigations.' He also said that the men had assured him they would complete the task within two weeks, but he insisted that it should be done by 23 January 1999 at the latest.[8]

Satya Prakash then contacted his nephew Pradeep Sharma to terminate Shivani and asked him to come to Sunder Nagar market on 19 January 1999. Satya Prakash, along with Sri Bhagwan, persuaded Pradeep Sharma to take the task. When Pradeep demanded a sum of ₹3 lakh in addition to favours, Sri Bhagwan gave him a sum of ₹50,000 as an advance. The deal was finalized with the go-ahead from R.K. Sharma.

When the evil plan was to be executed, R.K. Sharma made sure that he wasn't in town and had an airtight alibi. He was attending a Vertical Interaction Course for IPS officers at Central Institute of Road Transport (CIRT), Pune from 18–23 January 1999. R.K. Sharma later said, 'I was confident of my safe escape if anything untoward happened but I was slightly apprehensive of anything that would expose and drag me into the crime.' That's why he took the precaution of creating this strong alibi by getting himself sponsored for this course.[9]

While he was in Pune, his mind was in Delhi. Rather than use his own phone to keep in touch with Bhagwan, which would have raised suspicion, R.K. Sharma borrowed

---

[8]Ibid.
[9]Ibid.

a friend's mobile phone. Bhagwan was at an STD booth, relaying information between the execution team stationed outside Shivani's home and R.K. Sharma in Pune.

Satya Prakash, Ved Prakash and Kalu, along with Pradeep Sharma, scouted the area and hatched the plan. The task was to be done on 21 January 1999, as per the directions given by R.K. Sharma. However, they were unable to complete this as Shivani wasn't in her flat that afternoon.

On 23 January 1999, Pradeep Sharma was called outside the Mother Dairy stall in the locality. There, he was handed a box of 'besan ke laddu'. This box of sweetmeats were later used as a ruse to begin a conversation with Shivani. Ved Prakash and Kalu had been scouting the area since morning. They gave the green signal as soon as Pradeep Sharma and Satya Prakash arrived on the scene.

Pradeep Sharma entered the building, telling the security guard that he wished to go to Shivani's flat as he had a wedding invitation for her. He entered his name on the building visitor's entry register and proceeded to the flat with the box of sweetmeats in his hand. It was a 'friendly' entry. Using the excuse of the fictitious invitation card, Pradeep got Shivani to open the door for him. He even offered her the sweets he was carrying. As mentioned earlier, even though Shivani called her husband to inquire if he knew any Adhikari, it didn't help keep her safe.

∽

Even the most hard-core, cold-blooded killers are known to sometimes show compassion. At the very least, they try and make sure that they do not snuff out their victim's life in front of their children. Even the trained, albeit fictional, assassin Jason Bourne couldn't complete the assassination of African dictator Wombosi aboard a yacht after he encountered young children seated in the lap of his target. Children tend to have a kind of softening effect, even on the toughest among us.

But this was not the case with Pradeep. The former employee of the Haryana Urban Development Authority had no such qualms. Dismissed from his job on account of misconduct, Pradeep was now keeping himself busy doing odd jobs—errands for politicians and their lackeys; wheeling and dealing; and a bit of intimidation here and there for good measure. No job was too much for him, not even the ugliest and most cruel ones.

The Shivani Bhatnagar murder was another routine hit job for him. He would be paid handsomely for it, and an offer of getting his old job back also dangled before him. He demanded ₹3 lakh along with favours, including dropping of the previous cases against him. Pradeep, of course, didn't know who Shivani was or what she did. Until a few weeks before the murder, he didn't even know what she looked like. He probably preferred it this way. Most contract killers prefer to not know much about their targets or even why they are getting killed. As Alfred Lord Tennyson said, 'Theirs not to reason why, theirs but to do and die.' Professional killers simply can't afford to get entangled in the lives of their victims. They only study their victims for the purposes of knowing the best time to pounce, and get away without getting noticed.

Despite being in a business where even a small mistake can cost one heavily, Pradeep was quite clumsy. For one, he made no effort to cover his tracks. He left his fingerprints all over the crime scene: on the glasses, on the sweetmeat box and even on the kitchen surfaces. Maybe he didn't think that, with the connections he had, these details would ever come to haunt him.

Pradeep proceeded to stab and strangulate Shivani in front of her three-month-old son. Once the task was accomplished, the offenders informed Bhagwan on the phone. He then conveyed the same to R.K. Sharma in Pune. The latter then told them to come to Mumbai immediately, where they were to receive the payment and share the details of the execution of the plan. The following day, the trio (Bhagwan, Satya Prakash and Ved Prakash Sharma) reached Mumbai and procured the remaining contractual amount.

Call records from R.K. Sharma's phone revealed that no sooner had he stopped calling Shivani, the number of calls between his phones and the other co-accused had increased. It kept increasing right up to the date of the incident, post which the calls stopped suddenly. His protestations of innocence weren't enough to save him from arrest. R.K. Sharma was determined that if he was to go down, he would take the others with him. As news broke that the police were on the lookout for him, he first took a leave and then went into hiding. At that time, he was working as the inspector general of prisons of Haryana.

Even as he went into hiding, R.K. Sharma's wife began a tirade against the then Union Minister Pramod Mahajan. Suddenly, the identity of the biological father of Shivani's child was a matter that the 'nation wanted to know'. This was much before the days of rabid news channels. It was Mahajan, according to Madhu, who was responsible for Shivani's death and not her husband. She even demanded that Mahajan be subjected to a DNA test to prove that he was not the father.

But the charges against Mahajan soon flickered out. Years later, a phone tapping revealed a conversation in which a corporate lobbyist was heard speaking of how they 'managed' to save Mahajan from that case. Conversations between Anil Ambani and Satish Seth (29 January 2003) clearly revealed how Reliance was trying to manage the Shivani Bhatnagar murder case to favour Pramod Mahajan. They also talked about how the company was able to control the uproar in the Parliament by using Amar Singh.[10] What was the truth? Perhaps we will never know.

As the news cycle focussed on R.K. Sharma's disappearing act, his attempts to evade custody cost him his job and made him the country's No. 1 fugitive. But as his options ran out and he couldn't secure anticipatory bail, R.K. Sharma ultimately surrendered.

The prosecution believed it had a watertight case against R.K. Sharma. They kept the call record details at the crux of their arguments. Lawyers spent hours arguing. Initially, R.K. Sharma and the co-accused (Sri Bhagwan, Satya Prakash and Pradeep Sharma) were convicted and sentenced by the trial court to undergo life imprisonment besides being fined.

But in the Delhi High Court, they were given the benefit of doubt, and their convictions were overturned. The police were ultimately unable to prove that the call records were reliable enough to be the basis of conviction. Pradeep Sharma was convicted, as his fingerprints and handwriting were

---

[10]Jain, Meetu, 'The Rot Goes Deeper Than Radia', *Outlook*, 18 June 2016, https://bit.ly/3TDraxd. Accessed on 24 March 2023.

found to be conclusive enough to nail him for the crime.

The bench of Justices Badar Durrez Ahmed and Manmohan Singh said:

> We are of the view that exhibit PW135/28 is not a direct computer printout of the data available in the computers/servers of the telephone company. The impression we get is that the data as appearing has been tampered with. Certain details have been blanked out and others have been introduced. The date sequence and the time sequence has been altered as discussed above. These are clear indications of tampering/manipulation. On the basis of available evidence we cannot determine as to which part of the exhibit is authentic and which part isn't. We are also not clear as to whether the tampering was done at the instance of RK Sharma, who was a powerful police officer, or at the instance of someone else. The fact remains that the call records pertaining to the mobile phone number 98110XXXXX [which allegedly belonged to Sri Bhagwan] are unreliable.[11]

It left the court with a tricky situation—there was enough evidence to sustain the conviction of Pradeep Sharma, but he certainly didn't act alone. On the other hand, R.K. Sharma certainly had enough reason to kill Shivani but there wasn't enough evidence to link him to the crime. The crucial link between Pradeep Sharma and the other accused was broken.

The High Court ruled:

---

[11]Ravi Kant Sharma v. State, CRL.A. 357/2008, Delhi High Court, 12 November 2011.

Although the motive behind Pradeep Sharma killing Shivani Bhatnagar is unclear and has not been established, we have already found, on the basis of other overwhelming scientific and circumstantial evidence, that Pradeep Sharma was the person who killed Shivani Bhatnagar. Did he act alone? Did he act at the behest of RK Sharma and the other appellants or did he act at the instance of someone else? These are questions which we cannot answer on the basis of the material before us. The quality of evidence before us is not of a high caliber. The key document is riddled with so many problems that it cannot be relied upon. Judges, like other human beings, also have suspicions but, judges, unlike others who are free to arrive at their own conclusions, cannot and do not convict on the basis of mere suspicion. The prosecution has to prove its case beyond reasonable doubt. We are afraid that the prosecution, in our view, has failed to do so insofar as appellants RK Sharma, Shri Bhagwan Sharma and Satya Prakash are concerned.[12]

R.K. Sharma refused to discuss his guilt or lack thereof. He later stressed that it was time to 'move on'.[13] For Shivani's family, however, the scars will remain forever.

---

[12]Ibid.

[13]Rohtaki, Hina, 'Shivani Murder Case: I Believe In Moving on in Life, Says RK Sharma', *The Times of India*, 15 October 2011, https://tinyurl.com/3rxkcwvh. Accessed on 27 July 2023.

8

TILL DEATH DO US PART

The stalking and murder of Priyadarshini Mattoo[1]

It was a chilly January morning. At 9.15 a.m., Priyadarshini Mattoo left her home at Vasant Kunj (a plush neighbourhood in southwest Delhi) as per her routine. A student of law at Delhi University's Campus Law Centre, one of the most prestigious colleges in Delhi, Mattoo was a charming, energetic young girl. She had a deep commitment to righting wrongs, standing up against inequity and lived by the motto 'live every day like it is your last'. Except this day, 23 January 1996, was really her last. She, of course, didn't know it then as she set out from home for her university.

At 25, Priya—as she was known to her friends and close ones—had her whole life ahead of her. She was in the sixth

[1]Case details and quotes from: State (through CBI) v. Santosh Kumar Singh, Criminal Appeal No. 233 of 2000, FIR Nos. 50/1996, Delhi High Court, 17 October 2006; Santosh Kumar Singh v. State (through CBI), Criminal Appeal No. 87 of 2007, Supreme Court of India, 6 October 2010.

semester of her law degree; had parents who were academically and professionally accomplished; and a home in Vasant Kunj to count on. Priya had studied at the Presentation Convent in Srinagar and completed her bachelor's in Commerce from the Maulana Azad Memorial College in Jammu. She hailed from a family of Kashmiri Pandits—a community that had then been recently forced to leave their homes in the wake of targeted violence and even killings.

While those her age were enjoying the carefree days of youth, Priya could afford no such luxuries. Wherever she went, she was accompanied by a personal security officer—a head constable provided by the Delhi Police to ensure her safety. This wasn't because she was the daughter of a VIP or a person of high net worth. Her father Chaman Mattoo was the chairman of Sulabh International, while her mother Rageshwari Mattoo was an advisor with the NCERT (National Council of Educational Research and Training) in the government of Jammu and Kashmir. They were a well-connected family, with a commitment to work where they could make the most impact. They had decent jobs, no doubt, but not ones that would have primarily required their daughter to be given police protection.

The issue was that the young Priya was being stalked, persistently and with impunity, by Santosh Kumar Singh.

Santosh knew Priya, as he was her senior in law school. More importantly, he was the son of a senior police official. At that time, his father J.P. Singh was the inspector general of police in Pondicherry. As he was from the same IPS cadre that policed Delhi, he had friends in all the right places in the police establishment.

Santosh had graduated from college but continued to

hang around at the campus often making sure that Priya was aware of his presence. College life at the Campus Law Centre was like any other college. Students found their own cliques, friend circles and 'gangs' as they deluded themselves into thinking they were mafiosos. They would then carefully choose spots across the campus, which they would mark as their own territory.

For Arun Anand—Priya's batchmate who later went on to become a journalist—and his friends, that spot was Bunni Lal tea stall. It is here that college gossip would waft, waiting to settle on eager ears, becoming a point of discussion among friends and classmates.

Arun Anand later spoke about Priya in an article for Indo-Asian News Service (IANS), saying:

> ...I first heard a talk about a tall guy named Santosh Singh trying to woo a Kashmiri girl [...] Her first name, Priyadarshini, was not known to any of us; most of us just knew her as Mattoo. The general buzz was that Santosh and Mattoo had a casual conversation once or twice and the guy took it otherwise. And then the talk was that Santosh had been smitten by her charm.[2]

Priya was a person who was impossible to ignore. She was smart, beautiful and aced strumming a guitar. This was in an era when just being able to strum a few chords on a guitar would make one feel like a rockstar. Such was the novelty associated with this 'Western' musical instrument, that it was unlikely that any of her peers had even seen a

---

[2]IANS, "'Mattoo-Santosh Was Campus Gossip'", *News18*, 19 October 2006, https://tinyurl.com/ywpaub68. Accessed on 7 June 2023.

guitar first-hand before. Priya could actually play and sing along, mesmerizing those around her.

She absolutely loved playing the guitar. Music was an essential part of her life. She had even recorded herself reciting poems and ghazals on magnetic tapes. She had in her collection her own renditions of the famous works of Begum Akhtar, Faiz Ahmed Faiz, Ghulam Ali and, of course, Lata Mangeshkar.

Indu Jalali, Priya's friend who later became a leading crusader in the 'Justice for Priyadarshini' group, described her as such: 'A bubbly girl loaded with confidence...a tom boy, not at all submissive, and very compassionate towards animals.'[3]

As her friends recalled later, Priya had chosen to study law to fight injustice. She hated violence and injustice, and that's why she chose to become a lawyer.

Her father Chaman Mattoo, while writing for *The Indian Express* post her death, revealed:

Once, Priyadarshini even stalled a flight as she wanted to take her dog Snoopy along with her. The pilot said it was against aviation rules to allow anyone with pets on board. She insisted that there was no such rule in any lawbook which said dogs couldn't board a flight. The plane was stalled for two hours and she walked on board only after the pilot apologised and Snoopy was allowed to travel.[4]

---

[3]'Mattoo Birthday: Memories, March for Justice', *The Times of India*, 23 July 2006, https://bit.ly/3MfBaL0. Accessed on 11 May 2023.

[4]'I Weep Every Day Waiting for the Wheels of Justice to Move', *The Indian Express*, 22 March 2006, https://bit.ly/3I2k6FB. Accessed on 11 May 2023.

And then there was Santosh, who was quite the antithesis to Priya. Arun Anand in his IANS piece, wrote about Santosh saying: 'I had hardly seen him talking or mingling with other students in CLC. He was a quiet chap, had a small group of friends. He remained aloof, and at times appeared too quiet.'[5]

Arun further recalled:

> During those days there were often rumours that Santosh had proposed to Mattoo and she had spurned the proposal and snubbed him. We never knew what the truth was as rumours and gossip flying thick and fast were commonplace in the Campus Law Centre. [...] It often happens in university that friends tease you and pep you and tell you that a particular girl seems to have a soft corner for you. That was what probably happened with Santosh also. I thought he would soon realise that his friends were just trying to pull a fast one on him. There was often talk about how Santosh's friends had made him believe that Mattoo would respond positively.[6]

Whatever it was, it got into Santosh's head that he was deserving of her reciprocation. The otherwise shy, not very chatty guy developed a nasty streak. Perhaps it was his friends who egged him on, or perhaps it was the fact that they planted a seed of infatuation in his mind which then

---

[5]Anand, Arun, '"Mattoo-Santosh was Campus Gossip"', *News18*, 19 October 2006, https://tinyurl.com/ywpaub68. Accessed on 7 June 2023.
[6]Ibid.

took root. Perhaps, he took some of her actions to mean a reciprocation of his feelings for her and the more he thought about it, the more he felt he should 'have' her.

Many a time, a spurned proposal can bring a chapter to a close. The proposer gets so embarrassed by his gaffe that he slinks away in shame. At other times, the proposer tries to salvage the situation by promising to be friends and pretends the episode never happened. However at other times—and this happens more often than it should—the proposer simply thinks that the only reason he was rejected was because he just chose the wrong moment or didn't present himself well enough. They delude themselves by thinking that the girl is playing hard to get, or that she likes him but can't say yes just yet. He feels he isn't trying hard enough and wants to 'prove' his love by trying again.

One of the above or perhaps a combination of all of the above is what happened with Santosh. His attitude soon turned toxic and dangerous. It wasn't just hanging around the college campus and hoping to catch a glimpse of Priya. Nor was it limited to cat calling or passing lewd remarks as she walked past. It was much worse. He first began with accosting her when she was alone, then he went on to call her home landline and even followed her on his Royal Enfield Bullet.

Priya's requests and even pleading to stop only encouraged him further. Santosh's constant stalking didn't go unnoticed by Priya's parents. Her father later deposed that in December 1995, he noticed that Santosh and two or three more boys were passing lewd remarks at his daughter. Her mother too later testified that when she was admitted in AIIMS, Santosh was repeatedly calling Priya on the telephone despite the fact that she was not taking his calls.

∽

On 22 February 1995, when Priya was travelling in her car, Santosh followed her. When they stopped at a traffic light, he got off his bike and physically blocked her car. He even lay on the bonnet of the car, grabbed her car keys and made a nuisance of himself. This forced Priya to lodge a police complaint.

In her complaint with the R.K. Puram Police Station in Delhi, Priya said:

> For the last four months, I have been constantly harassed by a man named Santosh Kumar Singh who was a student in the Law faculty and has now finished his LLB. I have repeatedly asked him not to harass me but he persisted even to the extent of coming to my house at all odd hours. I brought this to the notice of my uncle, Col S.K. Dhar who also tried to reason with him.
>
> However, the man continued to persist in harassing me on every possible occasion in the Faculty (college) as well as outside. He started coming to the house when my uncle was away and I had to instruct the servant not to allow him in. My mother was in town earlier this month and she also tried to reason with him on one of the occasions.
>
> Today again, when I left the house at 10.30 am to go to my friend's place I found him following me and trying to stop my car at every traffic light, screaming and shouting at me to stop.

Despite this complaint, no action was taken against Santosh. He only got a warning that he shouldn't repeat his behaviour. This only emboldened him further. On Valentine's Day 1995, Santosh showed up at Lt Col S.K. Dhar's house. His house was at Safdarjung Enclave in New Delhi. The retired army officer was like a father figure to Priya and allowed her to stay there when her parents were away. Santosh came with a bouquet of flowers, which he handed over to the servant Bishamber with an accompanying card that read: 'Happy Valentine's Day - with love from Santosh.'

These incidents of harassment were confirmed by Lt Col S.K. Dhar as well, who later deposed that Santosh had been harassing Priya from November 1994 onwards and would repeatedly come to his house on his black Bullet when she was staying there.

In August later that year, Santosh followed Priya in her car right up to her residence and even tried to barge in. The police were called in and Santosh was made to give an undertaking that he would keep away from her. Priya was urged not to pursue her complaint, but she refused to comply. Her complaint was kept pending.

One isn't really sure what led Santosh to believe that Priya would actually end up being close to him despite everything he had done to harass her. What mindset is it that allows men like Santosh to actually believe that the woman will have no mind of her own? How did he think that she would simply submit herself to him because that is what he wants? Police officer Maxwell Pereira, who handled the case before it was handed over to the CBI, offered an explanation. In his book[7] penned after his retirement, Pereira said that the relationship wasn't as made out in the media. Priya and Santosh were in a 'deeply troubled love affair' and 'physically intimate', Pereira claimed. 'The relationship was vehemently opposed by Priyadarshini's family, though it appears Singh's parents went so far as to make overtures for a matrimonial alliance at one stage. Priyadarshini was hopelessly caught between her parents' wishes, a new and more promising alliance, and the increasingly irrational Singh,' Pereira said.

Perhaps it was Pereira's way of trying to explain why the Delhi Police were reluctant to take action against Santosh's clearly criminal behaviour. The police's inaction earned the ire of several judges who severely criticized the handling of the case.

Priya and her father met the commissioner of police, the top police officer in New Delhi, and complained against Santosh's behaviour and police inaction. The family was redirected to meet the deputy commissioner, who, after the customary patient hearing, rather than agreeing to take action against Santosh, assured that the police would offer Priya the services of a personal security officer. This policeman was to accompany her wherever she went and had to ensure that Santosh stayed away from her. This was all because they felt it would be easier to defend than eliminate the threat who, in this case, was the son of a senior police officer.

But like many efforts before this, this too was bound to fail. The presence of a police head constable made no

---

[7]Pereira, Maxwell, *The Tandoor Murder: The Crime That Shook the Nation and Brought a Government to Its Knees*, Context, 2018, pp. 251–52.

difference to Santosh. He continued to hang around the campus and her classes, staring at her whenever she walked passed. He even got his friends to 'reason' with her to agree to a 'relationship'.

It only earned him another complaint, which was lodged with the Maurice Nagar Police Station in Delhi on 6 November 1995:

> This is my third complaint (earlier complaints lodged at R K Puram and Vasant Kunj) regarding Santosh Singh, who has been harassing me for the last one year. Last week, I reported it to the higher authorities who have attached an PSO with me and asked to take immediate action against him if he indulged in such harassment again.
>
> Sir, today Santosh Singh chased me up to my classroom harassing me and forcing me to listen to him and catching hold of my arm as I was ignoring his threats when he tried to forcibly talk to me. I immediately called my personal security officer, he also told this to the police station. The police came and took him away when he tried to run away after seeing the PSO. He has been constantly indulging us forcibly asking me to talk to him and spoiling my reputation.
>
> Sir, he has also been using his friends' help in chasing me and threatening me on the campus and elsewhere.

This time Santosh was arrested but released on a personal bond that would be forfeited if he didn't change his behaviour. But again, it made little difference.

In retaliation, Santosh complained to the University management that Priya was pursuing two courses at once, which he said was against the rules. On account of this, Priya's third year examination results were kept on hold while the university authorities probed the complaint.

After Priya's death, the Supreme Court observed:

> It appears that as his overtures had been rebuffed by the deceased (Priya), [Santosh] had resorted to harassing her in a manner which became more and more aggressive and crude as time went by. It is evident that [he] was well aware of her family background and despite several complaints against him and the provision of a PSO, he had fearlessly and shamelessly pursued her right to the doorsteps of her residence ignoring the fact that she had first lived in the house of Lt. Col. S.K. Dhar, an Army Officer from the end of 1994 onwards and after January 1996 with her parents, her father too being a very senior officer in a Semi-Government Organization.

Every day was a struggle for Priya. The storm clouds seemed to follow her wherever she went. When her personal security officer, the head constable Rajinder Singh, told her that he would be late on 23 January 1996 to accompany her to college, she must have been extremely worried. He told her that he would instead meet her directly at the college campus where she was due to arrive.

That morning, Priya left her house with her parents who were to be dropped at the Tis Hazari Court Complex in

Delhi. She left home at 9.15 a.m., dropped her parents off at 10.15 a.m. and arrived at her college by around 10.30 a.m.

Head Constable Rajinder Singh arrived at the campus and noticed Santosh standing beside his Bullet with his helmet in his hand. Priya attended class from 11.15 a.m. till noon and left for home along with her PSO, checking on the way to see if her parents were ready to come home from the Tis Hazari Court Complex. Since they were not there, she proceeded towards home and by 1.30 p.m. she dismissed her PSO, asking him to return at 5.30 p.m.

At 2.30 p.m., her servant Virender Prasad too sought her leave and went out to meet his friend. He returned by 5.00 p.m. and then left to buy some medicines and also took the dog for a walk.

When her PSO Rajinder Singh returned at 5.30 p.m., nothing seemed amiss. He rang the doorbell and waited for someone to answer. At first, he thought that those inside the house might be resting and couldn't immediately come to the door. But as time passed, he began to worry. When there was still no response, he went towards the courtyard door and knocked, hoping that someone would respond. No one did. Since the door was a bit ajar, he pushed it open and went inside. Lying under the double-bed in the bedroom was a motionless Priyadarshini.

Rajinder Singh panicked and immediately used the nearest phone to contact the Vasant Kunj Police Station, breathlessly narrating what he had just seen. The police entry read:

> The time is 5.45 p.m. At this time HC Rajinder Singh
> No. 415/SW has informed on telephone from house
> No. B-10/7098, Vasant Kunj that he was the Personal

Security Officer of Priyadarshini Mattoo, daughter of Shri C.L. Mattoo... Priyadarshini Mattoo had called him for duty at her house between 5.30 pm. On arrival at the house of Priyadarshini Mattoo was lying under the double bed placed at the bed room of the house and there was no movement of her body. It appears that some incident has taken place...

A police team was immediately dispatched, led by Additional Station House Officer (SHO) Lalit Mohan. But it was already too late. Priya had passed away. She had been strangulated using a power cord of a convector, and there were blood stains all over her body. She was alone at home when she was attacked. There were ligature marks on her neck, and blood was oozing out of her mouth as she lay on the floor with very visible scratch marks on her mouth, neck and chest.

The post-mortem report found a total of 19 external injuries and three broken ribs. While the primary cause of death was certified as 'asphyxia as a result of strangulation', it was also opined that the injuries found on the body were by themselves sufficient to cause death. She wasn't just killed. She was battered and then strangled to death.

There were no eyewitnesses, but the post-mortem and evidence gathered allowed the police to piece together what might have happened.

༷

Priya's parents returned home at around 7.30 p.m., by which time a crowd had already gathered around her house and there was a commotion. Chaman Mattoo later described that time as some of his darkest hours. In an article in *The Indian Express*, he later wrote, 'My daughter's room in the house still remains untouched. It's the same as she had left it—cosy and warm. The room has her picture, on the shelves are books on Economics, Law and Commerce.'[8] This piece was published in 2006, a decade after her passing and the room was still intact.

The finger of suspicion of the murder soon fell on Santosh. Priya's mother Rageshwari in her statement to the police said that she believed it was Santosh who should be treated as the prime suspect. Based on her statement, he was called in for questioning. Since his hand had an injury, he was sent for a medical examination, which confirmed a fresh fracture in his right arm. He claimed that he had sustained the injury during a bike accident two weeks earlier.

But the evidence was piling against him. A neighbour, Kuppuswami, told the police that he saw Santosh standing outside the door with a helmet in his hand around 4.50 p.m. that evening. Jaideep Singh Ahluwalia, the security supervisor, had seen Santosh near Priya's residence at around 5.30 p.m.; while another witness, Advocate OP Singh, had seen him taking his Bullet out of the parking area.

Most importantly, Priya's servant Virendra Prasad saw Santosh there. Santosh had told him that he wanted to meet Priya to discuss a possible compromise regarding the withdrawal of complaints on either side. Prasad had then left the house to buy medicines and had also taken the dog out for a walk (as mentioned earlier).

---

[8]'I Weep Every Day Waiting for the Wheels of Justice to Move', *The Indian Express*, 22 March 2006, https://bit.ly/3I2k6FB. Accessed on 11 May 2023.

But Santosh feigned ignorance. Those were the days before CCTV cameras and mobile towers could be used to track individuals. Back then, even DNA forensics and profiling were cutting-edge technology and were used only in rare cases. These cases were usually the ones where police were groping in the dark to try and conclusively prove the presence of a person at a crime scene.

The murder case was promptly handed over to the Central Bureau of Investigation within two days of the incident, to help the family secure a free and fair investigation out of the reach of the accused's father. It was believed that J.P. Singh would try and influence the Delhi police to botch up the case and save his son.

⁂

As Priya faced her attacker, it must have became apparent to her that this time was different than the countless interactions she had with him before. The Delhi High Court, in its judgment, observed:

> He went inside the flat of the deceased and she being alone he did with her what he had all along been desiring to do i.e. to have sexual relationship with her and to put an end to the chapter once and for all lest he should be caught for that act, he assaulted her with his helmet and then strangled her to death.

Santosh first battered Priya with his helmet as she resisted the assault, then raped and strangled her. He struck her so brutally that he even fractured his wrist in the process. And when he was done, he quietly walked out and rode off. The brutality left even the judges of the High Court shocked.

Justice R.S. Sodhi later expressed in his High Court judgment:

> Why did the accused (Santosh) go to this extent agitates the mind. Why was he after the deceased? [...] The continuous stalking... in spite of police complaints, shows his utter disregard to the rule of law. [Santosh], it appears, did not care for the consequences and pursued his activities single mindedly [...] Either he would have her or make sure she did not enjoy her life. His activities do suggest a strong motive of 'do or die' attitude.

The recovery of the helmet with a broken visor, and the recovery of glass pieces from near the dead body, along with the fact that Santosh himself sustained injuries are some of the other things that conclusively prove the molestation and murder. Police officer Pereira suggested that Santosh, during his interrogation, 'confessed' that what happened in the room was what provoked him to murder her. Pereira said:

> The evidence is unequivocal that on the day of her killing, she had invited Singh to her home when he called her from a booth hear his university – telephone records confirmed the call. This despite the FIR she had lodged against Santosh for stalking. Priyadarshini didn't inform her personal security officer of her arrangement with Santosh Singh. She took pains to conceal his visit from her domestic help as well, sending him away to buy medicine and then to walk the dog so she could be with Singh at her home in private.[9]

---

[9]Pereira, Maxwell, *The Tandoor Murder: The Crime That Shook the Nation and Brought a Government to Its Knees*, Context, 2018, p. 251–52.

Pereira said that Singh defended himself by claiming that he and Priya had engaged in consensual sex at her apartment. However, when they were done, she asked him to withdraw his complaint with the Delhi University. This was something he refused to do. 'A pen and paper were found at the scene, which seemed to corroborate this claim,' Pereira said.[10]

According to Pereira, Santosh told the police that when he refused, Priya threatened to lodge a police complaint against him for breaking into her home and raping her. That was when he bludgeoned her with his helmet and later strangulated her with the power cord.

∽

On 3 December 1999, the court was to announce the verdict on the case. Chaman Mattoo was back in Jammu, having left Delhi after the tragic events of that day. While he was in Jammu, his wife had joined his elder daughter in Boston while his son had moved to Canada. It was only the Mattoo patriarch who had been left behind, and who had pursued the case with the help of friends and family while alternating between Jammu and Delhi.

The court's verdict was a killer blow to him. He later recounted:

> On the evening of December 3, 1999, I got a call from a newspaper editor telling me that the judgment in my daughter's case is out and Santosh Kumar Singh is a free man now. This left me absolutely dazed […] I could

---

[10]Ibid.

not sleep and I was jittery. Logic failed me because the circumstantial and scientific (DNA report) evidence had fixed guilt on the accused. [...] The judgment took a toll on me. I gave up my consultancy business as I could not concentrate on my work. I became a recluse. My wife insisted that I join her abroad but I withstood the pressure.[11]

The trial court, in a 450-page judgment after a trial that lasted three years—despite it being fast tracked and despite the overwhelming evidence—acquitted Santosh. The trial judge found all but one of the circumstances—the DNA test—to have been tampered with and decided in favour of Santosh. He was acquitted of both rape and murder.

The trial court did have some strong words for the role of the Delhi Police in how they handled the case. The judge noted:

The local police including officers of the rank of ACP had been helping the accused Santosh Kumar Singh at every stage in order to please [his] father who was a very senior police officer and also that if the police had taken the complaints lodged by Priya seriously she would have been alive. [...] It has also been observed that if in place of [Santosh], there had been any other ordinary citizen stalking [her] he would have been immediately put behind the bars but in the case of this accused he was simply let off everytime by the police after he tendered apologies and undertook not

---

[11]'I Weep Every Day Waiting for the Wheels of Justice to Move', *The Indian Express*, 22 March 2006, https://bit.ly/3I2k6FB. Accessed on 11 May 2023.

> to repeat his misdeeds which undertakings he never
> intended to honour and sometimes by persuading [her]
> to keep her complaints in abeyance.

The acquittal led to an uproar—not just on the streets but even in the highest echelons of government including Parliament. People were outraged at the failure of the country's justice system to give justice to the family of a girl raped and murdered. K.R. Narayanan, the then president of the country, even compared the courts to casinos in the wake of the judgment.[12]

Allegations were flying thick and fast. When the trial was still going on, an anonymous letter was sent to the Chief Justice of the Delhi High Court alleging that a trial court judge had been paid a handsome bribe to decide the case in Santosh's favour. The judge was then forced to recuse from the case after the letter became public and sparked a controversy of its own.

The CBI was forced into filing an appeal. But it was another seven years before the family would see the light at the end of the tunnel. There was a massive media-powered campaign called 'Justice for Priyadarshini'. The campaign reached a crescendo on what would have been her thirty-third birthday on 23 July 2006. A candlelight protest march was conducted at India Gate. The procession was attended even by Members of Parliament. Such was the impact of the campaign that it prompted the Delhi High Court to

---

[12]"Speech by Shri K.R. Narayanan, President of India, on the Occasion of Golden Jubilee Celebrations of the Supreme Court of India', *K.R. Narayanan*, 28 January 2000, https://bit.ly/3HWZvCv. Accessed on 11 May 2023.

take notice of the case, then lying in cold storage. Who knows what would have been the fate of the case had it not been for people like Indu Jalali and Aditya Raj Kaul, who championed the cause across various fora. The case was fast-tracked and heard every day.

Finally, the day arrived. Jalali later told the BBC, 'The credit goes to the media. They took up the case and kept the spotlight on, otherwise it would have continued to languish in the files.'[13]

∽

On 17 October 2006, the court declared: 'We are of the opinion that a case of this kind in which the crime is committed in a pre-meditated way and grotesque manner, the convict deserves nothing other than death penalty.' These words must have hit Santosh Kumar Singh like a shockwave.

Dressed in grey trousers and white shirt, Singh displayed no apparent sign of discomfort. It was all a daze and the events of 23 January 1996 seemed a really long time ago. The verdict was a culmination of a long and arduous battle for the friends and family of Priyadarshini Mattoo. But for Santosh's family, it was the opposite. Ever since his acquittal in 1999, Santosh went on to marry, father a child and set up a legal practice. Maybe it was for this reason that he was ultimately saved from the gallows.

It was another one year until the Supreme Court heard his appeal against conviction. The Supreme Court, while

---

[13]Pandey, Geeta, 'Justice Delayed, but Not Denied', *BBC News*, 17 October 2006, https://bbc.in/42pVFKl. Accessed on 11 May 2023.

upholding the guilty verdict, reduced the sentence from death to life behind bars. Supreme Court judges Harjit Singh Bedi and Chandramauli K.R. Prasad said:

> In particular we notice the tendency of parents to be over indulgent to their progeny often resulting in the most horrendous of situations. These situations are exacerbated when an accused belongs to a category with unlimited power or pelf or even more dangerously, a volatile and heady cocktail of the two. The reality that such a class does exist is for all to see and is evidenced by regular and alarming incidents such as the present one.

When he was saved from the gallows and his sentence was changed to life behind bars, Santosh told the *Hindustan Times*: 'I am feeling relieved. I am happy and satisfied.'[14]

A source from jail also mentioned: 'He was quite hopeful about being spared the noose though and would tell other inmates how he had been wronged.'[15]

His past haunted him as he continued to be in denial about his crime and brooded over it. As part of the obligatory labour to be undertaken by convicts, Singh runs the sub-jail's Legal Aid Cell that has three other inmates as members.

Priya's father later told NDTV: 'We are shattered and

---

[14]Nair, Harish V., 'Mattoo Family and Friends "Shattered", Singh Relieved', *Hindustan Times*, 7 October 2010, https://bit.ly/41mZa3b. Accessed on 11 May 2023.

[15]Sharan, Abhishek, 'Mattoo Killer is a Popular Legal Counsellor at Tihar', *Hindustan Times*, 7 October 2010, https://bit.ly/3nTh3sC. Accessed on 11 May 2023.

dismayed [...] We had expected better treatment from the courts [...] But the person who gave me the most strength was Priya herself.' [16]

[16]'Priyadarshini Mattoo Case: Supreme Court Commutes Death Sentence to Life', *NDTV*, 6 October 2010, https://bit.ly/3VYdgGX. Accessed on 11 May 2023.

9

MURDER BETWEEN THE SHEETS

The murder of IT professional Kaushambi Layek[1]

It's been more than 70 years since the Alfred Hitchcock classic noir-thriller film *Strangers on A Train* released, and yet it remains one of the most acclaimed movies of all time. It is a movie that continues to fascinate everyone even today. Unsurprisingly, the film went on to become critically acclaimed not only because of the fine work of Hitchcock, but also because of our fascination with meeting people by chance on a temporary journey.

It's a theme that has resonated throughout popular culture. A chance encounter with the right person, during an otherwise mundane journey, can have a profound impact on one's life. It offers the possibilities of new business partnerships, new employment opportunities or meeting

[1]Case details and anecdote from: Manish Naresh Thakur v. The State of Maharashtra, C.R. No. 251 of 2007, Criminal Appeal No. 454 of 2014, Bombay High Court, 12 July 2018; The State (at the instance of M.I.D.C.) v. Manish Naresh Thakur, C.R. No. 251/07, Court of Session for Gr. Bombay at Bombay, 4 March 2014.

one's life partner. These things are later labelled as what 'fate had in store'.

Kaushambi Layek was on one such train journey. She didn't know it at the time. When she boarded a train from her hometown (Dumka) to Trivandrum, she began a literal and emotional journey.

∽

Kaushambi Layek was 22. She had completed her MBA from Birla Institute of Technology, Ranchi, and also obtained a degree of MCA (Master of Computer Application) in 2005. She was on the train to Trivandrum to attend a training programme as part of a new job at Tata Consultancy Services (TCS).

As a brilliant student with a gold medal, Kaushambi was not short of offers after completing her graduation. So, when TCS came calling, she was ready. The bright, young girl was looking forward to an unstinted career in the IT industry that would take her places—from small town India to global cities. She embarked on a train journey, setting off into the world.

Indian train journeys have a life of their own. As the lifeline for the poor and the middle class, the railways help ferry millions of passengers every day. Strangers who share compartments make new friends, spend time playing cards, share snacks and life experiences while passing their time. Trains in India are never in a hurry to get to their destination.

Kaushambi was travelling with her elder brother, Shaunak, who had come along to ensure her safety. They were in a three-tier AC coach, and that's where things started to unfold.

Shaunak later recalled that they settled in for the night

at around 11.00 p.m., but when he woke up later that night, he noticed his sister talking cheerily to 'one boy'. The boy introduced himself as Manish Thakur, and said that he was headed to Kochi. Shaunak didn't make much of it then.

Manish was a 26-year-old sailor with the Indian Navy and was posted at the INS Garuda, Air Engineering Department in Kochi. His job was to coordinate and supervise the maintenance and repair of aircraft and helicopters. He had joined the Navy in 1999 and was first posted in Mumbai (on INS Kunjari) from 1999 to 2002. Later, he was posted at INS Shivaji at Lonavala for six months. Since then, he had been posted at Kochi as an aircraft technician.

Kaushambi and he were on the same train, as he too was heading back to his base from his hometown Kolkata.

Upon successful completion of her training, Kaushambi was posted to the company's Mumbai office at the Bandra Kurla Complex. Back then, Orkut was in vogue. While mobile phones and WhatsApp were a good few years away, the first buds of long-distance relationships, without keeping the landlines busy through the night, had begun to sprout.

Manish and Kaushambi were soon dating and, thanks to Orkut and chance meetings, the relationship blossomed. Kaushambi made no mention of her relationship to her friends. It was only in February 2007, almost two years after that train journey, that Kaushambi introduced Manish to her colleagues. She invited him to join them at the food court of the spacious TCS campus in Mumbai.

It is at the food courts of corporate India where the bonds between colleagues develop. It is here that colleagues get to gossip, make fun of each other and enjoy some time outside the tension-filled spaces of their office. But these food courts can also be spaces of awkward encounters, tense situations and embarrassing moments.

It was on one such awkward afternoon at the food court, that Kaushambi introduced the colleagues to her 'friend' Manish. Her colleagues politely acknowledged Manish.

Vipul Pathak (an office colleague and friend) and Kaushambi would often spend evenings together, either sitting by the sea face at Worli or watching movies together. They were close, but it was strictly a platonic relationship. Vipul later recalled how he was not particularly fond of Manish. He was taken aback to encounter a man who, despite being a big part of Kaushambi's life, was never talked about before. Vipul later took this up with Kaushambi, who sheepishly replied that she was having a 'love affair' with Manish.

While Vipul did not know a thing about Manish, the same was not true the other way round. Manish knew a lot about Vipul, including how close he was to Kaushambi. That even made him extremely jealous. He had already identified Vipul as a potential threat to his relationship with Kaushambi. He was so insecure that barely a month after they first met, Manish called Vipul and asked him to 'stay away' from Kaushambi. He said that he loved Kaushambi and nothing should come between him and his love. He also wrote an email to Vipul, claiming that Kaushambi was his life and that he wouldn't be able to live without her. In the email, he detailed how the two of them spent nights together in hotels in Mumbai (specifically mentioning Hotel Classic Residency).

Always the gentleman, Vipul reassured Manish that his relationship with Kaushambi was not a threat and that they were just friends. Vipul also reiterated his stance when he met Manish for the second time on 5 April 2007. Kaushambi reassured Manish that there was nothing between her and Vipul that was a cause for worry. Yet, nothing seemed to placate him.

For Kaushambi, the relationship began completely harmlessly and in a way that many can only dream of— by meeting a tall and handsome stranger. It made for an attractive, exciting encounter. However, this exciting encounter soon turned toxic.

Manish was hiding a dark secret—a secret Kaushambi had learnt of in the most mortifying way.

∾

A few months after Manish and Kaushambi met on the train, Shaunak received a call from a lady who identified herself as Nitu. The lady was insistent and claimed that she had something very important to discuss. During the conversation, she revealed that she was Manish's wife. She had got to know, she didn't say how, that her husband was having an affair with Kaushambi. Maybe she found a photograph of the two together, or maybe the photograph only confirmed something she long suspected.

Either way, Nitu warned Kaushambi's brother quite early on. It wasn't just Shaunak that Nitu called; she also called Kaushambi's aunt to try and keep her away from Manish. Nitu alleged that Kaushambi was responsible for her marriage not being consummated. She was trying to make her marriage with Manish work and blamed Kaushambi for scuttling her efforts.

Shaunak was extremely shocked when he got the news. In patriarchal families, a wayward daughter is considered a blight upon the family and the women are given very little choice in who they can talk to. Kaushambi's family was more liberal, but a scandal was not something they were prepared to handle. The only saving grace was that this affair was playing out in faraway Mumbai and, if kept under wraps, it would most likely not trickle back to their social circles back home. However, they couldn't take the risk. Kaushambi's family needed her affair to end quickly.

Shaunak was quick to relay all the information to his sister, along with the unequivocal message that whatever she was up to needed to stop. Kaushambi in turn, out of deference to her brother, assured him that she would bring their relationship to an end.

In most Indian families, a woman usually has no say at all even when it comes to their own lives and choices. This is true even if the woman in question earns more than the rest of the family members put together—which was the case with Kaushambi. She had lost her father to cancer a few years earlier, and her mother made ends meet by running a typing institute that, with each passing year, brought decreasing returns. Her brother had taken up the duties as head of the household, but it was Kaushambi who sent money to support her family. On her shoulders lay not just the weight of her own expectations but also that of her family's.

Kaushambi found her brother's instructions devastating. On the one hand, she was charmed and enamoured with Manish; but on the other, it was not a relationship that had a clear way forward. The distance between Manish and her didn't really help the case. Despite her brother's instructions, Manish and Kaushambi continued to date.

࿅

As mentioned earlier, Manish was posted at Kochi in a strict naval base setting, where Internet access was not easy to come by. It was only when Manish visited Mumbai that the two would get time together. The two usually spent the night in hotel rooms—Hotel Classic Residency at Andheri was their favourite. They even managed to make friends with the staff working there. Maria Paul Chettiar, the receptionist at Hotel Classic Residency, later said that he recalled Manish and Kaushambi spending the night in the guest house on at least two occasions—in March 2007 (when they spent two nights) and again in April 2007.

In February 2007, Manish was selected to undergo Pilot Simulator (Mechanical) Training in Moscow, Russia for MiG-29K aircraft. These were being procured for the Indian Navy to be onboarded onto the country's lone aircraft carrier, *INS Vikramaditya*. As part of his preparation to visit Russia, he was required to undergo Russian language training. On 24 February 2007, he left Kochi and reported at INS Hansa, Goa the following day. His posting at Goa allowed him to visit Mumbai more frequently. He visited Kaushambi over the weekends. The visits only helped strengthen Manish's resolve to try and convince Kaushambi to spend the rest of her life with him.

Manish had no plans of walking away. Kaushambi must have been torn apart by Manish's demands, her own reservations and her family's demands.

In April 2007, during one of his visits to Mumbai, Manish picked up the courage and decided to call Shaunak. He wanted to convince Shaunak that he was serious about Kaushambi. Manish even told Shaunak that he intended to marry Kaushambi and needed her family's approval. Shaunak did not tolerate any of it. He instead asked Manish how he planned on marrying his sister while already being married.

This turn of events clearly left Kaushambi distressed. With Manish's divorce not making any headway and his insistence on beginning a life together, she was caught in a bind. While she enjoyed spending time with him and liked him, she had her own doubts. She even confided in Vipul that as Manish was already married, she wanted to leave him. Bringing an affair to an end is not always easy, especially when one partner desperately wants to hold on to the other.

While Manish would not take no for an answer, Kaushambi was still wavering. She was being tugged in many directions. On the one hand, Manish kept insisting on formalizing their relationship; and on the other, her family had their own doubts about him.

∽

Towards the end of April 2007, Kaushambi made a visit to her hometown. She spent a few days there, between end April and early May. Though she was visiting for a housewarming party, she also used the time to catch up with her family. The issue of her relationship with Manish inevitably came up. When they learnt that she was still in touch with him, her aunt made her promise that she would never talk to or see Manish again. Kaushambi told her aunt that she would keep the promise.

Kaushambi's cousin, Kaushik Layek, later told the *Mumbai Mirror*, 'The whole week that she spent with us, she was happy and said she would like to move abroad as she had completed two years with TCS and could be put on online projects. She was an ambitious girl and we always encouraged her. She returned to Mumbai on May 7.'[2]

On 12 May 2007, a few days after she returned to Mumbai, at around 6.30 a.m., Manish and Kaushambi showed up at the reception counter of the Hotel Classic Residency. It was their third visit and by now they had become familiar with the hotel staff. Whether willingly or through coercion, despite the promises made to her family, Kaushambi was with Manish at the hotel.

Maria Paul Chettiar was at the reception. As fate would have it, the hotel was full that morning. However, Chettiar offered to check with hotels in the neighbourhood as a favour to them. He promptly phoned Hotel Sun and Sheel to inquire about the availability of rooms, and, on receiving a positive response, directed the couple towards it.

The couple reached there at about 7.30 a.m. and were allotted Room No. 202. The following afternoon on 13 May, a waiter took lunch to their room.

Later that night, at around 10.30 p.m., Kaushambi called her brother and told him that Manish wanted to marry her. Shaunak scolded her and asked her to come back home. However, he softened his tone on sensing that she sounded disturbed. Her tone changed, her voice sank and she began responding in slower and more measured words. He then asked her where she was, to which she responded that she was at her rented accommodation. When he asked her to pass the phone to her roommate Megha, the line went dead. Shaunak's attempts to reconnect

---

[2]Rajput, Rashmi, 'Manish Thakur Was Married', *Mumbai Mirror*, 17 May 2007, https://bit.ly/3nPzoqn. Accessed on 11 May 2023.

with her or with Megha proved futile.

That was the last time Shaunak heard from Kaushambi.

∽

At about 1.00 p.m. on 14 May 2007, Anup Lal, a senior staffer at the hotel, received a message from the reception counter that nobody was responding to the calls or opening the door for Room No. 202. The hotel staff were trying to get in touch with the couple, to ask them if they wished to extend their stay. Up to that point, no one in the hotel thought anything was amiss. With the couple mostly keeping to themselves and barely stepping out, it wasn't thought to be unusual. Besides, nothing was heard from the room that would suggest something was wrong. However, with them not getting a response, panic had begun to set in. Anup Lal asked the housekeeping supervisor, Robin Varghese, to check the room.

Robin opened the room using a spare key, and to his horror saw blood on the bed. He immediately called Anup and told him what he saw. Anup and Robin then went to the room and saw the mattress soaked in blood, and a blanket rolled up around a woman's body with her hair spilling out of the mattress. They shut the door and immediately informed their boss, who asked them to call the police.

Kaushambi was dead. As the police began inspecting the room and removed the blanket, her motionless body rolled out. She had been shot twice—first through her temple and then through her neck at point-blank range.

The police also found one cartridge lying below the cot towards the left side, and a knife was also found in the drawer of the dressing table. There was a purse and two bags. One of the bags contained ladies' clothes and the other contained gents' clothes. In the bag containing menswear, there was one white vest with letters written in blue 'SOUTHERN NAVAL COMMAND'.

While the police was summoning a dog squad and forensic experts to examine the crime scene, Manish was at the INS Hansa base in Goa, engrossed in his Russian class.

On 16 May 2007, two officers of the Navy walked into the classroom and escorted Manish out. They detained him and took him to Mumbai. His life as a free man was over.

For Kaushambi's family, the loss of their daughter was more than devastating. Her mother Ranjana and brother Shaunak had the unenviable task of travelling to Mumbai and performing her last rites. Kaushambi's death was more than they could take. After collecting the body, her mother conveyed to the media, 'Like any other parent, I wanted to see my daughter dressed as a bride. But we are preparing her body for the pyre instead.'[3]

Trying to make sense of the news, Kaushik said, 'She was not the kind who would go out with a person like Thakur. This person (Thakur) is a psycho and he must have been stalking her.'[4]

After five days of interrogation in Mumbai, Manish broke down and offered to show the Mumbai Police the location of the murder weapon. The next day, at around 7.00 a.m., he

---

[3]Ibid.

[4]"Love on Net Ends with Murder in Web of Deceit', *The Indian Express*, 17 May 2007, https://bit.ly/3LPAxX0. Accessed on 11 May 2023.

led a team of the Mumbai Police, along with the officers of the Indian Navy, to a building in INS Hansa. He proceeded to take them to the roof. After removing the roof tiles, he removed a polythene bag in which two country-made pistols and some ancillary equipment was kept.

Manish had left so much evidence behind that even his attempts to claim an alibi, saying that he was back at the base when the murder took place, did not convince the court of his innocence. The fingerprints from the crime scene matched with the ring finger from his left hand; the used bullet that was recovered from the room matched with the gun that he had handed to the police; and his name and address on the hotel guest register left no doubt that it was he who had murdered Kaushambi.

Everything pointed to a pre-planned murder and not one that took place in the heat of the moment. His decision to carry not one but two pistols and a chopper knife with him that weekend indicated that he had only one thing on his mind—murder. However, all of the evidence all over the place pointed towards it being a crime of passion. Manish came across as very clumsy for a pre-planned murderer.

∽

On 4 March 2014, almost seven years after the murder, the Additional Sessions Judge D.W. Deshpande pronounced Manish Thakur guilty of the murder of Kaushambi Layek and sentenced him to life imprisonment. His appeal against the verdict was also rejected by the High Court. In jail, Manish met and befriended Emile Jerome (a Navy officer who was convicted of murdering his fiancée's boyfriend Neeraj Grover. He had chopped the body, stuffed it in a suitcase and burned his remains).[5]

There was only one thing that flummoxed the police, the courts and observers alike—the motive. Why would a man who clearly claimed to have loved his girlfriend, and even told her friends that he couldn't live without her, kill her in cold blood? After all, if he was willing to murder, wouldn't it have made more sense to murder his lawful wife? She was persistently refusing divorce. Wouldn't it have made more sense to get rid of the 'obstacle' that was in his way?

What happened in the room during their stay is known only to them. Manish chose not to testify before the court and claimed an alibi of having spent the weekend back at base, playing cricket with his mates. He even got a few of them to testify that he was with them. He also got a bank manager to claim that he met him back at the base to discuss some investment proposals. Neither claims found favour with the court, as when an accused claims alibi it is for him to conclusively prove that he was indeed where he said he was—which Manish was not able to do.

There was another clue that later emerged. Dr Mahadev Bansode, the one who conducted the post-mortem examination, said that there was no evidence of sexual intercourse found for the last four to six days before Kaushambi's death. The trial court judge said, 'It means that the deceased was keeping herself away from the accused in the room. The above evidence would demonstrate that the deceased wanted to keep away the accused. So as the

[5]Zaidi, S. Hussain, 'Two Jail Mates Helping Salem Write His Story', *Mumbai Mirror*, 22 November 2014, https://bit.ly/3NZR8tO. Accessed on 11 May 2023.

deceased refused to marry with the accused or wanted to keep herself away from the accused, Kaushambi was murdered.'

Perhaps, Manish thought that Kaushambi wasn't being truthful to him. This insecurity, coupled with an inability to stomach her increasing reluctance to carry on with the relationship, could be what pushed him to do this deed. It could also be her closeness to Vipul that he did not like. Kaushambi was in constant touch with Vipul via her newly acquired mobile phone, when she spent two weeks back in Dumka.

Stuck between Manish and her family's expectations, Kaushambi's desires and opinions seemed to matter very little to either of the two parties. It was a tug-of-war and she was the rope. Probably enraged at the turn of events and perhaps even doubting her fidelity, Manish pulled the trigger, killing Kaushambi instantly.

Police suspect that Kaushambi was murdered around 10.45 p.m. on Sunday, shortly after her call with Shaunak. Manish left the hotel immediately without collecting his belongings, so nobody would suspect him. Her body was found only the following afternoon.

Would things have ended differently had Shaunak relented and given his consent to the union? That's a question that only Manish can answer. But what we can say for sure is this: Kaushambi lost her life because the people in her life, who believed that they were best placed to decide what's good for her, couldn't see eye to eye.

10

AN UNHOLY TRINITY

Sex, murder and coverup in a Kerala convent[1]

It was three days before Christmas in 2020 when Biju Thomas received a call that he had been anxiously waiting for since morning. Based in Dubai, far removed from his home state Kerala, Thomas was closely tracking a trial that had begun in 2019. It was a trial that went down as the longest trial in India's history—with the judgment set to be delivered more than 28 years after the crime took place.

Fifty-one years old and living far away from home, Thomas couldn't help but be taken back to the events of 1992. He was then in Gujarat, studying a hotel management course. While at the hostel, he had received a telegram through which he had got to know that something 'unfortunate' had happened to his sister, Abhaya, and that he should return

---

[1]Case details and quotes from: Central Bureau of Investigation, ACB, Cochin v. Father Thomas Kottoor and Sister Sephy, SC No. 1114/2011, C.P. No. 2/2009 of CJM, Ernakulam in R.C No. 8 (S)/1993/CBI/KER, In the Court of the Special Judge (Spe/CBI), Thiruvananthapuram, 2020; Sr. Sephy v. Union Of India, Bail Appl. No. 7311 of 2008, In the High Court of Kerala at Ernakulam, 2009.

home as soon as he could.

He later told *The Print,* that his first thought was that there had been an accident.[2] It was when he arrived back home and was asked to visit the mortuary that the real horror of what had happened dawned on him.

Biju Thomas hailed from a family of Knanaya Christians, an endogamous ethnic group found among the Christian community in Kerala. This group's history dates back to the earliest days of Christianity. The community traces back to the arrival of the Syrian merchant Thomas of Cana who led a migration of Syriac Christians (Jewish-Christians) from the Middle East to India in the centuries after Christianity emerged. The community settled down and flourished as part of the larger Syro-Malabar Christian community in Kerala. Closely knit and deeply respectful of their religious leaders, the Knanaya Christians have deeply ingrained religious and cultural traditions. Rarely does anyone dare to violate the written and unwritten laws of the community.

The Christian community of Kerala is one of the biggest contributors of priests and nuns to the Christian community in India. It has also been instrumental in sending missionaries abroad. In fact, in Christian religious institutes across India, chances are you will find a fair few priests and nuns who originally hail from Kerala.

---

[2]Swamy, Rohini, '"Instead of Warning, They Silenced Her"–Kerala Nun Abhaya's Brother Recalls 28-year Fight', *The Print,* 27 December 2020, https://bit.ly/3BdXTAO. Accessed on 11 May 2023.

The Thomas family was no different. While Biju didn't really feel the 'call' to serve in the 'vineyard of the Lord', his sister Beena Thomas was cut from a different cloth. In an interview with *The Print*, he said:

> When I asked her to reconsider her decision to become a nun... She said she wanted to help people and the only way was to dedicate herself to Christ and learn the scriptures. [...] I was quite naive then. I asked her to finish her religious studies and come back home to get married. She laughed and told me that once she becomes a nun, there would be no turning back.[3]

Beena had joined St Joseph's Religious Congregation to become a nun, at their hometown in Kottayam. She was staying at the St Pius X Convent Hostel while pursuing her studies at the Bishop Chulaparambil Memorial College (BCM College). She was one of around two dozen nuns for whom the convent was home. Upon her investiture, she took the name Sister Abhaya (meaning brave).

Convent life is even more sombre and rigid than a strict girl's hostel. Nuns in a convent usually have a fixed timetable, which involves a lot of prayer, daily chores and study time (for nuns who were also students). Contact with the outside world remained minimal.

The St Pius X Convent Hostel was an impressive five-storey building with larger-than-life religious imagery adorning its outer walls. Sister Abhaya shared a room with Sister Sherly, Sister Chyara, Sister Dhaya and Sister Anand on the ground floor of the building. They had to use common

---

[3]Ibid.

toilets. For drinking water, they had to go down to the cellar.

Sister Abhaya stayed in Room No. 8. Room No. 9 was occupied by Sister Anupama, Sister Sudeepa, Sister Salomi and Sister Naveena. Room No. 10 was occupied by Sister Suseela, Sister Smitha Jose, Sister Priya and Sister Kochurani. The cellar hosted common areas, like the dining room, the kitchen, a work area, etc. It also hosted a single bedroom that was occupied by Sister Helen, who was the mess in-charge, and Sister Sephy. The kitchen staff—Ms Achamma, Ms Thressiamma, Ms Regi and Ms Saino—stayed in a room on the ground floor.

∽

On 26 May 1992, at around 5.45 p.m., Sister Abhaya, along with a few other people from the convent, went to attend a Bible convention at Nagampadam, Kottayam. They returned to the convent by 8.30 p.m. They had their supper as usual at the refectory—a simple dinner of *kanji* (boiled rice in water) in keeping with their austere lifestyle—and went to the chapel for prayer before retiring to their rooms.

That night, Sister Helen was away in Kallara for a 10-day meditation course. This meant that Sister Sephy was the only occupant of the entire cellar floor that night.

After the dinner was over, Sister Sephy returned to the kitchen with a *kooja* (a narrow-necked pot) to draw water from the well outside. Ms Regi also accompanied her. They fetched water from the well and returned, closing the door behind them. Sister Sephy then took the filled kooja and went to her room. The kitchen staff then retired to their rooms, after taking her leave.

On the ground floor, Sister Sudeepa asked Sister Sherly

(Sister Abhaya's roommate) to wake her up at 2.30 a.m., so that she could study until dawn. Sister Abhaya also asked Sister Sherly to wake her up at 4.00 a.m., so that she could study. Sister Sherly set her alarm clock for 2.30 a.m. and when it beeped, she went and woke Sister Sudeepa up. She then went back to sleep. When the next alarm beeped at 4.00 a.m., Sister Abhaya heard it and woke up on her own. Sister Sherly, while half asleep, knew that Sister Abhaya had already woken up. She told Sister Abhaya to go ahead and study on her own. Crucially, she told Sister Abhaya to not go to the kitchen to get herself cold water since the kitchen staff were yet to rise.

Sister Abhaya, being the diligent student that she was, began studying on her own with the available light. After studying awhile, she went to the next room and woke up Sister Anupama. The two studied for about 15 minutes before Sister Anupama decided to go back to sleep.

While this was going on upstairs, on the floor below, two men were prowling about the convent premises, accompanied by a nun. The two men were later identified as Father Thomas Kuttoor and Father Jose Poothrikkayil. The former was a lecturer of Psychology at BCM College. The latter was a lecturer of Malayalam at BCM College and also the manager of the Catholic Mission Press.

But the movement of the two men, who thought they were sufficiently hidden under the cover of darkness, didn't go unnoticed. Perched outside the convent wall was the petty thief Adackka Raju. He specialized in stealing metal scrap and then selling it. This is how he sustained himself. Raju was waiting to enter the convent premises, so that he could steal the metal from the lightning rods. Raju later testified that on prior occasions he had entered the campus of the hostel, and climbed onto the terrace of the convent building to steal scrap metal. He had gone there on three occasions to steal the copper plates positioned on the lightning rod on the terrace. He would usually climb the coconut tree behind the compound wall of the convent, scale down it and enter the campus of the convent. He would then climb up the steps of the fire escape to the terrace of the building, break the copper plate from the lightning rod and hide it in a drainage channel, about 1–1.5 km away from the hostel. In order to kill time until morning, he would then lie on the veranda of the Government Hospital, Kottayam, until 6.00 a.m. or 7.00 a.m.

Later, in his testimony, Raju said: 'I committed theft on the terrace of that building for two days continuously and on the third day, I found two persons standing on terrace and watching the nearby areas with the help of torches.' In his testimony before the court, he later claimed that he recognized one of the men as Father Kuttoor. 'I know Father Kuttoor,' he told the court. On seeing the two men making their way through the fire escape, Raju was forced to bide his time. Raju's testimony proved crucial in the court.

∾

At around 5.00 a.m., Sister Sudeepa went and rang the convent bell for everyone to wake up. The bell was not just for the nuns of the convent but also for the kitchen staff, who promptly woke up and began their duties for the day. Ms Achamma, Ms Thressiamma, Ms Regi and Ms Saino woke up and made their way to the kitchen. Ms Achamma was the first to make it to the kitchen that morning.

What she saw left her troubled. The light in the corridor leading to the kitchen was on. This was surprising, since they had switched off all the lights before going to bed. She then went to the wash basin beside the kitchen and found the door connecting the kitchen to the wash basin area open, despite it being shut the previous night. The fridge door was ajar and a bottle of water lay on the floor, with water spilling out of it.

By then, others had also reached the kitchen. Ms Regi noticed a lone slipper lying near the fridge, while Ms Thressiamma found that the door leading from the kitchen towards the well was locked from the outside. Ms Regi clearly remembered that they had locked it from the inside last night. A white veil was found lying under the door, with half of it on one side of the door. They also noticed a small hand axe and an empty fruit basket lying overturned, with the fruits strewn about the floor. But there wasn't a drop of blood anywhere.

What could have happened while they were asleep? Had there been a scuffle? Had rats been playing about with the fruit? But how could rats bolt the kitchen door from outside? Had it been burglars who tried to grab a quick bite from the kitchen?

Ms Thressiamma was the first to postulate that the slippers belonged to Sister Abhaya. Ms Achamma asked Ms Regi to inform Sister Sephy about what they saw. They thought that she might have heard something at night, as she slept on the same floor.

Sister Sephy asked Ms Thressiamma to go to Sister Abhaya's room and call her. Thressiamma went upstairs and, after looking for Sister Abhaya in her room and in the chapel, came back to the kitchen and informed Sister Sephy that Sister Abhaya was missing.

Sister Sephy then informed the convent superior of what they had noticed in the kitchen. Since she was still in her nightgown, Sister Sephy stopped at Sister Susheela's room to borrow her habit (religious garment) and changed into it.

While changing her dress, Sister Sephy also informed the others present about what had happened. Mother Superior Sister Lisieux joined the others in the kitchen once she got the news.

Sister Lisieux, along with Sister Merlin and Sister Sephy, then went out to search for Sister Abhaya with a torch, as it was still too early in the morning for sunlight. They then came to the kitchen side and searched there but could not find her anywhere. They continued their search on the terrace by climbing through the emergency staircase. They even searched for her near the well, but she was nowhere to be found.

The first clues to where Sister Abhaya might be came from the bucket near the well, which Sister Sephy noticed was hanging close to the pulley. Since she was the last to use the well the previous night, she remembered placing the bucket on the ground.

By this time, all sisters who were residents of the convent had assembled in the kitchen. Nuns were deputed to inform the bishop as well as Sister Abhaya's family about her disappearance and soon enough, there was a fairly large group of concerned people trying to figure out where she could have gone. Each one took a look at the various clues, but none seemed to offer any explanation. Her father

Mr Thomas had also come over and was very worried.

Finally, Sister Lisieux decided to call the police. Accordingly, a complaint was lodged with the West Police Station, Kottayam, by Sister Lisieux at 9.15 a.m. on 27 March 1992.

∽

Additional Sub-Inspector V.V. Augustine, who was in charge of the police station that day, accompanied the nuns back to the hostel along with two or three other constables. Sister Lisieux took Sub-Inspector Augustine and his team to the kitchen and showed him what they had found.

Owing to the suspicions that Sister Abhaya might have fallen in the well, given the unusual placement of the bucket, they decided to look into the well. P.T. Mathew, who lived just across the boundary wall neighbouring the convent, brought some labourers and asked them to get into the well. They were instructed to dive in and look for anything resembling a body. They returned to the surface, saying that they had suspicions about a body being there, but they couldn't say for sure since the visibility was poor.

Sub-Inspector Augustine then approached the local fire department. They sent expert divers into the well. These divers fished the body out with the aid of a fireman's chair knot. The body was then laid beside the well before being photographed and sent for a post-mortem. It was, indeed, Sister Abhaya's body.

∽

Varghese Chacko was a photographer working for Kottayam Venus Studio at that time. He took photographs of the body using his Minolta 35-70 Zoom Lens camera, as per the instruction of the Kottayam West police. His photographs revealed nail mark injuries on either side of Sister Abhaya's neck. These became the first clue that she might have been choked during a scuffle. Those injuries were easily visible in the photographs.

For Sister Abhaya's family, this point was the start of a gruelling and heart-wrenching wait for answers concerning her death. Meanwhile, the circumstances surrounding the death sparked many conspiracy theories and hearsay.

With no one willing to come forward and no proper clues, the police were in the dark. The unenviable task of solving the case fell squarely on the shoulders of Sub-Inspector Augustine.

As a diligent police officer, Augustine went about registering the death as an 'unnatural' one and sent the body for post-mortem after it was photographed. The post-mortem found six ante-mortem (prior to death) injuries on the body. These included two lacerated injuries on the back of her head, which were possibly made using a sharp instrument.

Over the course of the next two days—27 and 28 March 1992—Augustine did considerable work for the investigation. He questioned as many as 24 witnesses, mostly those who were present in the convent when the incident happened. In his last diary entry for the case on 28 March 1992, he recorded: 'Maybe, Sr. Abhaya would have witnessed something objectionable on the crucial morning and somebody who would have felt that he was identified by her would have done something to cause her death and dumped her in the well...and this fact cannot be denied/disputed.'

Augustine's interactions with the convent residents and staff offered hints that there was an outsider, maybe more than one person, present in the convent during the wee hours of the morning. It is possible that she caught them, causing them to eliminate her. The lacerated wounds on the back of her head suggested foul play. The talk of errant priests and nuns indulging in forbidden sexual acts, usually consigned to pointless gossip, suddenly became relevant.

The theory that she was murdered soon seeped out, causing a public uproar. It led to protests and calls for justice. Owing to the uproar that had now engulfed both Church and state, Sub-Inspector Augustine was promptly removed from the case and the matter was handed over to the Crime Branch of the Kerala Police.

Although Augustine stopped working on the case two days after the murder, the Crime Branch officially took over the case nearly three weeks after. The delay was due to official red tape. For the next six months, they attempted to get to the bottom of the issue—or so the public was made to believe. Instead, they were in for a rude shock when in its report on 30 January 1993, the Crime Branch ruled Sister Abhaya's death as a 'suicide'. Crucial evidence was said to have been destroyed during this period, and the witnesses were either silenced or threatened.[4]

It was indeed surprising how the Crime Branch could arrive at the 'definite' conclusion that it was a case of suicide, when nothing that happened so far was pointing in that direction. It was this, more than anything, that gave

---

[4]Varghese, Joel, 'No One Killed Sister Abhaya', *ResearchGate*, January 2021, https://bit.ly/3O11zNF. Accessed on 11 May 2023.

the movement for justice its biggest impetus. It was now clear that a cover-up was being attempted. Else, the Crime Branch could simply have said that there wasn't evidence to say how she died. Instead, they actively put out a false theory that ricocheted back on the role played by the Church and the police.

Jomon Puthenpurackal, a human-rights activist, established and led the 'Sister Abhaya Case Action Council'. Puthenpurackal accused the investigating officials of botching up the case under pressure from the Knanaya Church. There were protests, political gatherings and delegations that went right up to the then Prime Minister P.V. Narasimha Rao in her support.

Following popular pressure and a legal battle launched by Puthenpurackal, the High Court of Kerala transferred the investigation to the Central Bureau of Investigation (CBI) in 1993.

∽

The case then remained with the CBI for another 15 years, with 13 different officers attempting to get to the truth. Suspected persons were subjected to lie detector tests, brain fingerprinting and other tests. The CBI attempted to recreate the scene of what might have happened that night. They even put out a public notice offering a reward for anyone who could come forward with credible information about the case. There was no response. In 1996, 1999 and in 2005, the CBI submitted three closure reports. The first one stated that there wasn't enough evidence to even say that it was a murder, and reported back saying that the evidence was inconclusive. The second one said that while it could be confirmed that it was a murder based on a medical inspection of the body, there wasn't enough evidence to nail anyone. The third report, by which time it appeared that even the CBI was fed up, said the same thing as the second report but using a different set of words.

None of the three reports were accepted by the judicial magistrates who, either out of public pressure or out of some nagging hunch, kept sending the reports back. They asked the CBI to keep looking. In 2008, the Judicial Magistrate Court directed that the case be handed over to the Kerala branch of the CBI.

Once this was done, seemingly out of the blue, the CBI claimed to have cracked the case. The first arrests were made shortly after the Kerala Branch of the CBI took over. They were finally able to piece together what they believed had transpired on the night of the murder. Here's what the CBI Kerala said happened. Father Kuttoor and Father Poothrikkayil had an illicit relationship with Sister Sephy, and used to visit her occasionally at the convent. On that fateful night with Sister Helen being away, Sister Sephy was the lone occupant of her room.

A little after midnight, the two priests arrived at the convent on Father Kuttoor's scooter. They then parked the scooter outside the compound wall, and entered the premises by scaling the boundary wall. They entered the kitchen room with the help of Sister Sephy and spent the night there. They were in the hostel until at least 5.00 a.m.

During the wee hours of 27 March 1992, Sister Abhaya came to the cellar floor to fetch water from the refrigerator. According to the CBI, Sister Abhaya saw the three in a compromising position, following which they chose to attack her in a bid to silence her. The prosecution put forth a case that Sister Abhaya was strangled by Father Kuttoor and struck on the back of her head by Sister Sephy. The three of them then dragged Sister Abhaya out and dumped her in the well. She was most likely semi-conscious at that time.

After this arrest, the case was fought for another 12 years. But on 23 December 2020, Special CBI Judge K. Sanil Kumar pronounced Father Kuttoor and Sister Sephy guilty of having murdered Sister Abhaya. This concluded the longest trial the country had seen. They were sentenced to life imprisonment. However, this sentence was suspended by the Kerala High Court in June 2022 while the appeal against the conviction is still being heard. Father Poothrikkayil was discharged in the case, owing to lack of evidence against him.

൦ൟ൦

For Biju, the verdict given in 2020 was a case of better late than never. But it came with a tinge of bitterness, as his parents didn't live to see the day when his sister's killers were convicted. He believes that if the perpetrators had simply asked her to keep quiet, she would not have defied them because that was not in her nature. In an interview with *The Print* after the verdict was delivered, Biju said, 'Those monsters took her innocence for granted and instead of warning her...they killed her.' He felt that they had finally received their due from God.[5]

---

[5]Swamy, Rohini, '"Instead of Warning, They Silenced Her"–Kerala Nun Abhaya's Brother Recalls 28-year Fight', *The Print*, 27 December 2020, https://bit.ly/3BdXTAO. Accessed on 11 May 2023.

But the conviction and the investigation itself remained surrounded by a lot of ambiguity. According to the thief Adackka Raju, he was tortured by the Crime Branch to admit that he was the one who killed Sister Abhaya. He had refused to falsely testify to save the priests. Raju told the court that the Crime Branch officials had asked him to admit to committing the crime, and said that a large sum would be sent to his family if he did so.[6]

Besides Raju, it was Jomon Puthenpurackal who deserves a share of the credit for relentlessly pursuing the case even at the risk of losing his life. Through the Sister Abhaya Case Action Council, he put pressure on the criminal justice system to ensure that her case was treated as a murder and not sought to be hushed up as a suicide. In 1994, his brother Uthuppan attempted to murder him causing serious wounds. Owing to timely medical care, the murder attempt didn't cost him his life. Puthenpurackal still believes that this attack was planned by the powerful Knanaya Catholic Church diocese of Kottayam.[7] The Church had been doing everything possible to bury the Sister Abhaya case and Puthenpurackal was perceived as a 'potential trouble maker' by them.

ço

[6]Joseph, Neetu, 'How Abhaya Case Witness Adakka Raju Was Subjected to Inhuman Torture by Cops', *The News Minute*, 25 December 2020, https://bit.ly/3pu1yIa. Accessed on 11 May 2023.

[7]Sreejan, B., 'Sr Abhaya's Death Case: Won't Rest Until the Appeals are Disposed, Says Jomon Puthenpurackal', *The Times of India*, 23 December 2020, https://bit.ly/3puqbo7. Accessed on 11 May 2023.

The CBI, in a sweeping allegation, said that the church was trying to hush up the case. However, the Catholic community strongly supported Sister Abhaya and wanted her to get justice. At the initial stages, when the Crime Branch sought to close the case as suicide, a complaint was signed by Sister Banicassia, Mother Superior and 67 other nuns of Congregation of Mother of Carmel. This was the same congregation to which Sister Abhaya belonged. Two visiting nuns even asked the then Chief Minister to entrust the investigation to CBI, alleging it to be a case of 'murder'. It was part of the reason why the state government transferred the case to the CBI.

Nevertheless, it goes without saying that the biggest indictment of what had happened that night was provided by the Church itself, in its attempts to destroy evidence in the case. R. Krishnakumar, a columnist, observed:

> Another factor was the rather awkward contrast between the response of the Church authorities to the sudden and mysterious death of a young nun, one of their own, and their perceived eagerness to be satisfied with the suicide theory, to come out with all their might in support of the accused priests and nuns at every instance [...] Right from the day Abhaya's body was discovered, the lukewarm response of the Church authorities had led to speculation on the alleged activities involving residents of the hostel and certain powerful forces.[8]

---

[8]Krishnakumar, R., 'Twists & Turns', *The Frontline*, 2 January 2009, https://tinyurl.com/4avxsx5a. Accessed on 7 June 2023.

This point is further backed by the fact that nearly all those present in the convent on that fateful night either turned hostile witnesses or pushed forward the suicide theory, almost in unison. It was a theory that was also put forth by Sister Sephy in her defence. She claimed, 'As her mother was suffering from mental illness, Sister Abhaya was under pressure and suffering from psychological depression. She came from an economically weak family and she was not good enough in her studies and these could be the reasons for her suicide.'

But the court was not impressed. The CBI Court Judge K. Sanil Kumar observed:

> A person bent on ending her life, and ending it in the immediate future at that, would not worry about her academic prospects, would not deny herself sleep for the sake of improving her examination performance, and would not devote herself passionately to study, much less engage herself in combined study with her fellow students. This single fact is sufficient to blow the suicide theory sky high [...] Sister Abhaya was a very smart, pious, honest, simple, perseverant and punctilious girl, meticulous in all aspects, leading an altruistic life and that it was simply impossible for her to have ended her life on her own as portrayed by the defence.

∽

While presenting the suicide as the truth, the opposers of the verdict also attacked the CBI investigation. The CBI was accused of drawing up a charge sheet based on hearsay and without any evidence to even prove that the two priests were present in the convent that night. Besides the testimony offered by Raju (who claimed to recognize Father Kuttoor in the dim starlight, making his way to the terrace via the fire escape) and Sanju P. Thomas (the neighbour who claimed that a scooter belonging to Father Kuttoor was found near his house at about 12.30 a.m.), there was no evidence that the priests were indeed in the convent on that night.

Detractors found support from the fact that some questions still remained, even after the CBI presentation. What were the priests doing on the terrace with torches if their intention was to quietly and clandestinely visit Sister Sephy? Why were they not looking to make a quick getaway doing their best to go unnoticed, given the illicit nature of their visit?

Sister Sephy was also put through a 'virginity' test, and accused of hymenoplasty by the CBI. Whether Sister Sephy was a virgin was completely immaterial to whether she murdered Sister Abhaya. The Delhi High Court in February 2023 ruled that subjecting Sister Sephy to a virginity test was unconstitutional and allowed her to seek compensation. Her plea against the conviction read:

> After assuming that A1 (Kottoor) and A3 (Sephy) were present in the convent kitchen at about 4:30 am, the court assumed they were having sex there... the court assumed Sr Abhaya happened to witness it. Then the court assumed that A1 and A3 hit Sr Abhaya on the head with a weapon (hatchet). The court further assumed Abhaya fell unconscious. The court lastly assumed that A1 and A3 threw her alive

into the well. This is how it convicted the accused of murder.[9]

As per the post-mortem, the two lacerated injuries on Sister Abhaya's head were less than an inch in length and not even skull deep. Blood was seen oozing out from the head even after the body was extricated and kept outside. If the contentions of the CBI are to be accepted, there should have been blood on the veil, the floor or on the weapon. There must have been at least a drop of blood somewhere in the area.

The High Court, which was hearing the bail pleas, said:

> But, in spite of the fact that Sr. Abhaya sustained two bleeding injuries on the head, no blood was seen by anybody on the scene, veil or the weapon which was found nearby. Not even a drop of blood was seen anywhere near the scene. If there was some blood, some inmate or a witness would have noticed it. Sixteen years of investigation, no body is alleged to have stated that any drop of blood was seen on the veil or the scene or the weapon. CBI could not point out any scrap of paper which reveals that any witness saw any drop of blood at the premises.

In another severe critique of the CBI investigation, Sub-Inspector Augustine poisoned himself to death and left a note blaming the CBI for harassing him. He was being forced to turn approver in the case, and to tell the courts

---

[9]'Abhaya Murder Case: Sister Sephy Moves HC Seeking Suspension of Sentence', *OnManorama*, 12 February 2021, https://tinyurl.com/vp4nms5z. Accessed on 7 June 2023.

that he was forced to destroy evidence. His diary entry from 21 November 2008 clearly states that he was being pressurized by the CBI officers. He was threatened with dire consequences and was reminded that it was not the Kerala Police that was dealing with the case anymore. He was told that if he didn't comply, he would be taken into CBI custody for 14 days. He died by suicide in November 2008 at the age of 62.

The brain fingerprinting investigation report by Dr Mukundan, done in 2003, indicated that there was a scuffle between Sister Abhaya, Sister Sephy and the kitchen staff. He did not elaborate on the cause of the scuffle. The report said:

> The test findings support experimental knowledge that the kitchen area was disturbed during a struggle with the deceased by Thressiamma and Achamma, Sephy and Sr. Shirly (who is Sr. Abhaya's roommate). The related probes depicted that Thressiamma and Achamma had helped Sr. Shirly from preventing Sr. Abhaya from running out of the kitchen. Sr. Shirly had first-hand information of the disturbances in the kitchen, as she too witnessed the scene. (She was the only person who was found visibly upset during testing); the possibility of Sr. Sephy personally involved in the murder of Sr. Abhaya was tested but findings did not support theory and on an investigation done on the various inmates of the hostel on the condition of Sr. Abhaya, there was overwhelming indication that Sr. Abhaya was depressed before her death.

The brain fingerprinting report could not be used as

evidence in the court, and one cannot easily dismiss the possibility that the findings of the test were tampered with. The theory put forth by the reports also didn't answer one question: If some of the residents knew that Sister Abhaya had 'jumped' in the well after the scuffle, why were they 'searching' for her all over?

What clearly emerged from this investigation, however, was the role of the Church in meddling with the investigation. According to Kemal Pasha, former Kerala High Court judge, who spoke to *The News Minute*, despite the conviction, Sister Abhaya can never get justice, 'not because of delay by the judiciary but because the church she believed in, fought for her murderers, and not for her'.[10]

After the trial was completed in 2020, a message, supposedly from the superior general of a nunnery, was circulating on social media platforms. In the post, the mother superior asks other sisters to chant a particular prayer 13 times to get a verdict 'in their favour'. The prayer was not for the justice of Sister Abhaya.[11]

Sister Jesme, a writer and retired college principal at St Mary's College in Thrissur, left the Congregation of the Mother of Carmel in 2008. Even she, in an interview with *The News Minute*, agreed that it was the church that failed Sister Abhaya. She said, 'The church will not tolerate any

---

[10]John, Haritha, 'Sister Abhaya Murder Case: Is it Really Justice Delivered?', *The News Minute*, 23 December 2020, https://bit.ly/3I17K0s. Accessed on 11 May 2023.
[11]Ibid.

accusations against them. They don't support the victim. We have seen that note seeking prayer from the superior general. They never worried about justice for Abhaya.'[12]

The many twists and turns at the various stages of the case were further complicated by the heavy media coverage. The Kerala High Court, which heard the bail applications of the priest and the nun, seemed convinced that this was a fit case of the investigating agencies (as well as the judicial magistrates) merely bowing to public pressure fuelled by conspiracy theories pushed forth by the media.

The High Court noted:

The media has pronounced the verdict already... The public has also joined hands, being carried away by the various publications effected through media, which do not contain the bare true facts which are revealed by the case records. A damoclean sword of a threat of ill-repute is held over the head of any judge who may ever dare to lift his/her pen and write or speak anything contrary to the 'media-public verdict' which is already pronounced. The three persons are already sent to the gallows. Then, why does the system of criminal justice exist anymore in this country? Many investigators, various officers of local police, Crime Branch, the 'church', the 'convent' and several others, dead and alive, are all in the dock. Even after the death of certain witnesses, allegations by the media and public still haunt them [...] Poor public. They do not know what the records bear. By the sustained brain washing on them, they may not be

---

[12]Ibid.

able to even accept any judicial pronouncement, which may run contrary to what they are made to believe so far. Honestly. The courts can go only on the basis of the facts covered by the case records. But, the public still chases the mirage...

Fortunately, for the Thomas family—of which Biju is the only surviving member—the trial court was sufficiently convinced to give a guilty plea. Judge Sanil Kumar, while quoting judgments from the Supreme Court in his final flourish, said: 'Proof of guilt is sustained despite little infirmities, tossing peccadilloes and peripheral probative shortfalls. The "sacred cows" of shadowy doubts and marginal mistakes, processional or other, cannot deter the Court. Justice would fail not only by unjust conviction of the innocent but also by acquittal of the guilty for unjustified failure to produce available evidence.'

'I am ready to die today. My mission is complete,' Jomon Puthenpurackal told reporters who surrounded him at the CBI court compound, after the priest and nun were pronounced guilty.[13]

Biju Thomas and Jomon Puthenpurackal weren't the only ones celebrating the verdict. An unlikely hero also emerged in the case. It was none other than Raju, whose testimony was all the court ultimately had to clinch the case. He said:

My child got justice. I wanted justice for her. She got it now, and I am extremely happy. I'll drink in joy today. I was offered crores. I did not take it. I still live in a

[13]Sreejan, B., 'SR Abhaya's Death Case: Won't Rest until the Appeals Are Disposed, Says Jomon Puthenpurackal', *The Times of India*, 23 December 2020, https://tinyurl.com/bdethxye. Accessed on 14 July 2023.

colony on three cents of land. I have two daughters. What happens if they are taken away from me one fine morning? I saw that child (Abhaya) like my daughter.

The matter has now reached even further with Father Kuttoor and Sister Sephy (71 and 57 at the time of their conviction), appealing against the order. Perhaps the truth will never be known in this case, except that Sister Abhaya was dead beyond question.

11

RED HOT RAGE:
THE TANDOOR MURDER

The shooting and brutal disposal of budding
politician Naina Sahni[1]

On the warm evening of 2 July 1995, Naina Sahni poured herself her favourite drink—an improvised version of a Bloody Mary cocktail. She substituted the tomato juice with tomato soup and added Tabasco sauce and vodka. As she settled down for what she thought was another tense evening, she hoped to distract herself by watching a movie. It was warm outside, but within the sparsely furnished flat, it was cool. Her apartment was the only one in the building that boasted of an air conditioner.

Naina found herself at a crossroads. There was much she wanted to look forward to, but life wasn't going exactly as planned. Just shy of 30, Naina felt it was time for her to take the 'next step'. Till this point, life had worked out

---

[1]Case details and quotes from: State v. Sushil Sharma, Delhi High Court, 19 February 2007.

quite well for her. She had come from humble beginnings but had reached the level of general secretary of the Delhi Pradesh Youth Congress (DPYC). She had a private flying licence, something most people her age and disposition could only aspire to have. She also ran her own fashion boutique that was well received by her high-profile customers. Yet, she had that gnawing feeling that there was more to look forward to.

The daughter of a storekeeper at the Army Ordnance Depot and a physical trainer in a West Delhi school, Naina had by all accounts had a middle-class upbringing. She had enrolled at Delhi University's Shyama Prasad Mukherji College and promptly entered student politics. It was a choice she had consciously made, and it came to define much of her life.

Student politics of the day, especially in Delhi, was often prone to violence and underhand tactics. This was during the 1980s, when the Congress was at its zenith, having successfully recovered from the setbacks caused by the Emergency barely a decade earlier. With Indira Gandhi having come back to power, the Congress ruled with almost unparalleled power through much of the '80s—the time when Naina was in college.

Naina's decision to enter student politics came as a surprise for her family. It's difficult to say whether she joined politics out of a genuine liking for it, or simply because it gave her something to do in a generally difficult time. The rather conservative family of Sikhs had no real connections to politics, and would generally keep a low profile. This was also the time when the brutality and horror of the 1984 anti-

Sikh riots of Delhi were all very real for the community. In this atmosphere, a member of a Sikh household joining the Congress party was pretty much seen as a taboo. It wasn't long before she was forsaken by her family.

But she wasn't one to be bogged down. She used her newfound freedom and political connections to help her get things moving. She took to swimming, then gliding and joined the Safdarjung Flying Club. This was where she finally earned a private flying licence.

Student politics often involved late hours, organizing, planning and running errands for political bigwigs. However, it also brought its own set of alliances and dalliances. And Naina—the pretty, ambitious and bright-eyed young woman—was not short of suitors.

Her first serious relationship was with Matloob Karim, who was also associated with the National Students' Union of India (NSUI). Karim was elevated to the post of general secretary of NSUI in 1984 and was sharing space in the committee with Naina (who was then the convener of the women's wing).

As the relationship between the two blossomed, Naina moved in and lived with Matloob for about four years. They ultimately separated amicably after Matloob chose to marry within his own community.

It was around this time that Naina became involved with Sushil Sharma.

∾

Sushil Sharma was also a fellow Congressman and president of the DPYC. He held this post between October 1989 and January 1995. Sushil was no ordinary man. He did not chance upon becoming the president of the DPYC. He was a formidable politician who was aspiring for a Lok Sabha ticket from one of Delhi's constituencies.

Sushil was a senior to Naina by about seven years, and hailed from the walled city of Old Delhi. His family originally hailed from Bulandshahr in Uttar Pradesh. He took to extracurricular activities during his school and college days.

Back then, one needed to be notorious to be noticed by a political party. And that was one department in which Sushil excelled. To call him and his friends bullies would be an understatement. Beating, threatening, confinement, kidnapping and other dubious tactics was Sushil and his 'gang's' forte. But to make it to the NSUI, he needed to go beyond just mere tactics.

Sushil learnt this the hard way when he ran for the post of the vice president of the Delhi University Students' Union. He came third. Rather than sulking at his defeat, he used the opportunity to only further his notoriety. Upon declaration of the results, he pulled a knife on the winning candidate Amitabh Roy of the Students' Federation of India (a Left-leaning students' federation).

Buoyed by his growing notoriety, Sushil ran for elections again and this time used even more brazen tactics—threatening to kidnap his rivals, attacking them or generally warning them of grievous harm if they didn't withdraw their candidature. Being the dominant figure that he was, many chose not to run against him and he emerged victorious.

Among the more notorious deeds done by Sushil was the stabbing of a rival candidate to death (conducted by members of the NSUI). But for some reason, Sushil managed to avoid being named an accused in the case. He soon had a string of cases against him, ranging from assault, grievous assault and threatening. However, owing to his political connections, the cases never amounted to anything.

Sushil and his gang would barge into the offices of the Delhi Police, manhandle constables, create a ruckus—all in the name of conducting a political protest. The real intention was to browbeat the police into showing them the light arm of the law. Whenever they were involved in their nefarious activities, they would get the police to turn a blind eye. They were sometimes involved in activities that they didn't really want the police snooping into.

Sushil became president of the DPYC in 1989, by which time he had made a long list of enemies. After more than five years in the NSUI, he proved to be very useful to the Congress party. He defended the government on the streets, to ensure that the bandh calls given by the Bharatiya Janata Party (BJP) were not fruitful. If the BJP youth wing would try and threaten shopkeepers to keep their businesses shut, Sushil and his men would ensure that they were sufficiently warned to do the opposite.

But it wasn't all muscle. In the eye of the public and the media, Sushil made sure that he maintained the image of a god-fearing man. This was perhaps because he had ambitions to go beyond being someone who only did the dirty work. It must have been a conscious decision to never be seen smoking, drinking or womanizing. Whenever he visited a temple, he made sure that he did so in front of the media. But it was all a facade. The reality was very different from the image he maintained.

❧

Sushil grew close to Naina during the time he was the DPYC president. She was then the general secretary. The two got married in 1992 in a strictly private ceremony. It wasn't even attended by Naina's family. Only a few of Sushil's family members made it to the wedding. It was a conscious decision to keep the wedding low-key. Aside from opposition from Naina's family, Sushil also didn't want the world to know that he was marrying her. The reasons for this were unclear but perhaps he felt it would hurt his carefully crafted image of being a god-fearing social worker who cared for the poor and the downtrodden. Perhaps, he feared that marrying someone who was not exactly an ideal model of a *sanskaari* wife would harm his political chances. The High Court later suggested that he must have been 'apprehensive also that he might lose the support of his followers and the sympathy of the public in general in case it became known to everyone that he was living with a fellow female leader of the youth'.

Naina moved in with Sushil at an upmarket flat in Delhi's DIZ area. After that, Naina kept a low profile. She slowly withdrew from her political activity and focussed only on being Sushil's wife.

Naina's family later described her as a 'dutiful housewife', in a note they circulated to the media after her death titled, 'The True Story'. The note read:

> Naina had to stop at the second rung of the ladder of her political career, because she fell in love with Sushil Sharma. His pre-condition to marriage was that Naina should stop all her political activities and forget about her political aspirations. She agreed...

As a dutiful housewife and daughter-in-law, Naina was like any other ordinary Indian wife. She had put her political career and ambitions behind her. Her parents-in-law whenever they called her parents spoke well of her good nature. She used to fast on karvachauth in the traditional way. And whenever she visited her own parents she always came accompanied by her husband Sushil. Both of them always looked happy and contented.[2]

This kind of married life must not have been easy, especially for a girl like Naina, who wanted to pursue her ambitions. In Naina's case, things were especially complicated because Sushil liked to show who's boss. He was used to having his way in the political field and expected to be treated with a similar mixture of awe and fear when he returned home too.

But Naina wasn't that type of girl. She was neither in awe of him, nor did she fear him. It was not without reason that she had come so far despite being a first-generation politician. Having left her family behind to join politics, Naina was pretty much left all on her own when things started to go sour with Sushil. He would mistreat her, and would even instigate his parents to scold or sometimes even physically abuse her.

Not only would he beat her in alcohol-fuelled bouts of anger, he would also lock her at home and even prevent others from meeting her. Sushil's cook too confirmed the beatings. The cook also talked about Naina's insistence that Sushil make the marriage public. Sushil ensured that she

---

[2]Pereira, Maxwell, *The Tandoor Murder: The Crime That Shook the Nation and Brought a Government to Its Knees*, Context, 2018.

was virtually a prisoner in his home, and if she did venture out, she was accompanied by someone he knew.[3]

Naina couldn't turn to her own party leaders for help or protection either, as within the party Sushil was just too powerful. He once drew his revolver, which he used to carry everywhere with him, on a fellow DPYC vice president (there were 14 of them). Even then, no action was initiated against him despite the woman in question having complained to party leaders. Keeping this in mind, what chance did Naina have of taking up a complaint of domestic violence with the party leadership or even the police?

For a while, Naina suffered in silence, but she knew she deserved better. She expected more from their relationship. Matloob Karim later told the police that despite the two parting ways, Naina would confide in him about Sushil's violence towards her. Matloob's presence in her life led to further problems. Sushil would always confront Naina over her insistence to continue being friends with Matloob. Things took a serious turn when Naina discovered that Sushil himself was involved in an on-and-off extramarital affair with Ila Jhunjhunwala. She was a woman from the upper echelons of society, whom he had known for a very long time. Upon learning of Sushil's philanderous ways, which were narrated to her by Ila herself, Naina decided she wouldn't take the abuse lying down. She decided to

---

[3]Ram Niwas Dubey, identified as a personal servant of Sushil Sharma in the court judgment, where his testimony is paraphrased.

give it back to Sushil and point out his own shortcomings.[4]

It was a counterpunch that took Sushil by surprise. As he was not used to being talked back to, it came as a rude shock to him. He must have hated that it was coming from someone who, according to him, was to be in his control. It was an ego that was badly bruised. And things had begun to rumble under the surface.

Naina would lament to a few friends, especially Matloob, about the violence she encountered, both physical and verbal. A note found by the police in their apartment throws light on how fraught things were between the two:

> Sushil, I know you hate me. You cannot accept me, so do not waste your time. Take care of yourself and forgive me. Leave me to my fate. We cannot continue like this because I cannot win you [sic] confidence even by killing myself. Take away whatever you have to. Don't misunderstand me. Do not let your life be spoiled. I know I do not deserve you. Leave me and me [sic] the best from your life. But do not say anything to my family. They are innocent. If you want to, you can punish me.[5]

The note was apparently written as a suicide note, or so Sushil later claimed. He had ripped it up, but the police pieced it together during the later investigation.

∽

---

[4]Jahargirdar, Archana, 'Sushil Sharma and Naina Sahni: A Relationship Fated to End Unhappily', *India Today*, 31 July 1995, https://tinyurl.com/5n863ff3. Accessed on 14 July 2023.

[5]Pereira, Maxwell, *The Tandoor Murder: The Crime That Shook the Nation and Brought a Government to Its Knees*, Context, 2018.

It was under these circumstances that Naina poured herself a drink on 2 July 1995. The couple had been sparring for weeks. With Naina growing increasingly indignant with Sushil, she realized that there was no future for them. She had begun making plans to move to Australia, where she wanted to start a new life and open her own boutique. The boutique she was running in Delhi after withdrawing from student politics was doing reasonably well. She was confident that she would do well in Australia too.

That evening, in order to pass her time, she called a video renting library to deliver two movies. She also called Matloob to inquire whether he had followed up with the travel agent who was tasked with securing her a visa for Australia. He assured her that he would follow up with the agent over the next few days.

Sushil returned home at around 8.15 p.m. that evening, and instantly the mood in the flat was tense. Naina offered him a drink, but they barely spoke.

The boy from the digital library arrived with the two video cassettes. It wasn't his business to figure out what was going on between the two—not that he would notice anything amiss. Little did he know that he would be the last person, besides Sushil, to see Naina alive.

Sushil was going through a lot at the time, but nothing consumed him more than the 'insolence' displayed by his wife. He had begun to doubt Naina's fidelity and had started keeping tabs on her. He would fly into a rage against her at the slightest sign of perceived defiance, which had become frequent.

Sushil realized Naina had been on the phone with someone when he arrived home. When he asked her who it was, she lied saying that it was a family friend. Sushil picked up the receiver of the phone and redialled the number. Back then, while we couldn't retrieve the entire call history, it was possible to trace the details of the last number dialled from the phone. He recognized the voice at the other end of the line as Matloob Karim. Already on edge, Sushil flew into a rage. He confronted Naina over why she continued to stay in touch with Matloob.

Naina coldly replied saying that it was none of his business.[6] Hearing this he stormed into the inner room and pulled out his revolver. He loaded it with four bullets, paced out and promptly discharged three bullets in Naina's direction in an act of rage. Two of the bullets pierced Naina's head and neck. The third missed, hitting a plywood board that stood behind her. She flopped to the floor, dying almost instantaneously. That wasn't even the most outrageous and evil thing that Sushil did that night.

Sushil later spoke to *Midday*, saying:

> That day, when I came home around 8 pm, Naina was speaking on the phone. The moment she saw me, she hung up. When I enquired, she said she was speaking to her mother. I already suspected that she was having an extra-marital affair with her ex-boyfriend Matloob Karim. When she went inside to get me a glass of water, I redialled and Matloob picked up the call. I panicked and confronted her.[7]

---

[6]Pereira, Maxwell, 'Tandoor Murder Case: How Sushil Sharma Killed His Wife Naina Sahni and Disposed off Her Body in a Restaurant', *DailyO*, 28 March 2018, https://tinyurl.com/5y56puc7. Accessed on 14 July 2023.
[7]Khan, Faizan, '"Had I Not Committed the Crime, I'd Have Been a Union

He also told *The Hindu*:

> That night, after the phone call, we fought and shouted at each other and I went out to the balcony. She then said she was going to commit suicide and also wrote a note. My gun was lying in the cupboard and I heard a gunshot. I went in and she said she wants to end her life. I said 'what rubbish,' after which arguments started again and then everyone knows what happened.[8]

The madness, rage, burning jealousy and seething anger that had been rumbling under the surface had finally erupted. Consumed by his passionate anger, Sushil killed Naina. For a while, Sushil had entertained the idea of murdering his wife. His initial plan, at least that's what he told the police, was to throw her off a cliff during their planned trip to Himachal Pradesh. However, with their relationship having deteriorated, Naina had kept stalling on the trip.

After murdering his wife, Sushil barely spent a few moments dwelling on what he had just done. His mind immediately went to how he should dispose of the body.

At first, he thought he would dispose of it in the Yamuna. He wrapped the body in a plastic sheet, carried it to his Maruti 800 and drove off in the direction of the

Minister Today"', *Midday*, 21 July 2019, https://bit.ly/3I1v9Pu. Accessed on 11 May 2023.

[8]Bhandari, Hemani, 'Tandoor Murder: I Regret Murdering Naina Sahni, Says Sushil Sharma', *The Hindu*, 22 December 2018, https://bit.ly/3I3KSgR. Accessed on 11 May 2023.

river. However, to his dismay, at around 9.00 p.m., traffic on the way to the river was much too heavy for his liking. This made it likely that he would be caught in the act. This forced him to think of another plan.

That's when he remembered the Bagiya Barbeque Restaurant at Ashok Yatri Niwas in the heart of the city. The eatery had a large enough tandoor oven that he could use as a makeshift pyre, to completely reduce his wife to ashes. Ghastly as it may sound, that's what he decided to do.

∾

The India Tourism Development Corporation, which ran the Ashok Yatri Niwas, had given the contract of running the restaurant to a private firm (Excel Hotels Inc.). Sushil was one of the five joint owners of the firm. With this connection, Sushil promptly phoned the restaurant's manager Keshav Kumar and asked him to vacate the restaurant that was still crowded with guests enjoying their evening meal.

Keshav was confused. Being loyal to his employer, and perhaps also afraid of him, he had no choice but to comply. He later pleaded guilty before the court in the hope of an easier sentence. He said:

> I was serving in the Bagiya restaurant of Sushil Sharma. On 2.7.95 in the night about 9/10pm Sushil Sharma came and said to me, 'close the restaurant'. I said, 'Customers are eating food. Let them eat'. Sushil Sharma said, 'Have you not heard what I have said to you? Do what I am saying!' I put off the lights of the restaurant at the instance of Malik [owner]. Then he [asked me] to take out the bundle from the

car. At that time Sushil said to me, 'I have murdered Naina. Immediately she is to be burnt in Tandoor.' I got perturbed and continued to do as Sushil said. Sushil said: 'Do what I say!' [...] Sushil Sharma put the dead body in the Tandoor and asked me to bring butter to raise the fire and put wood in the tandoor so that the dead body is burnt. On account of fear, I got more perturbed. I helped Sushil in the burning of the Tandoor at his instance [sic].

Sushil must have believed that he had gotten away with it. Naina had no one to speak up for her—her family had long abandoned her, and her friends could have been rebuffed and said that it wasn't any of their business if she was 'missing'.

As the body was burning, Sushil, in a rare candid moment, confessed to Keshav Kumar that he had erred in murdering his wife. They continued to add more fuel in the form of Congress party pamphlets, campaign material and logs of wood that were kept around.

∽

If not for the hard-nosed determination of a Delhi policeman, Naina Sahni's story would have ended there. Abdul Nazeer Kunju was on a double shift that night. It was a little before midnight when he was on his rounds along with Home Guard Chander Pal, when he noticed an unusually large fire at the restaurant attached to the Yatri Niwas. When he first went to investigate the fire, he was told that this wasn't a fire that was out of control but one that was deliberately set up to burn waste paper and other paraphernalia. He was told to not worry about it.

Little did he know that what was about to unfold would be among the most important events he would ever encounter. His statement to the police, which was later produced in court, is worth reading in full.

> At about 11.25 in the night I, along with DHG Chander Pal, while patrolling the area reached the side lane of Ashok Yatri Niwas. I noticed a woman and two-three other men crying: '*hotel mein aag lag gayi! aag lag gayi!*' I saw that from the wall side of Ashok Yatri Niwas, inside Bagiya Bar-be-que restaurant there was smoke and flames of fire. I wanted to telephone 100 and also fire brigade from the telephone booth stand installed there. But the telephone booth was closed. I left DHG Chander Pal at the site and rushed to the police station and fire brigade to the wireless picket which was on the back of Western court and nearby. From there with the aid of wireless I informed police station Connaught Place and from the CPWD inquiry of the Western Court I telephoned PCR and fire brigade. I returned to the site after about 20 minutes. The flames and smoke had increased.
>
> I entered the Bagiya Bar-be-que restaurant Along with DHG Chander Pal from the back. I saw a young man whose name now I have come to know [is] Keshav Kumar.... On the Tandoor of the restaurant there were big-big wooden logs, small wooden pieces of logs, he was pouring[9] on the Tandoor and was increasing the

---

[9]Word is missing from the original quote in the judgment copy. It could mean pouring butter or simply adding to the fire. The original testimony was in Hindi and a translation is in the judgment.

fire by reversing (stoking) the wood with [a] bamboo. I said to Keshav Kumar, 'By [doing] this the hotel would also be burnt.' Keshav Kumar told me, he is a worker of the Congress party and was burning the old posters, banners and waste papers of the party. Foul smell was emanating out of the fire.

In the meantime, patrol officer SI Rajesh Kumar, PCR Head Constable Majid Khan, Constable Rajbir Singh and security staff of the hotel Rajiv Thakur, security guard Mahesh Prasad etc. also reached. At that time adjacent to a kanat installed at the gate of Bagiya bar-be-que, a young man whose name security guard Mahesh told [sic] Sushil Sharma and the owner of the restaurant, was standing.

An associate of Sushil Sharma who had a healthy body, middle height and was wearing blue coloured printed shirt and pants was also there and another young boy well built, middle height was also present in the restaurant towards the side of Tandoor. With the aid of buckets containing water the fire was doused.

Because a foul smell was emanating out of the fire a suspicion arose to me and also SI Rajesh. Keshav Kumar was detained at the site itself, then along with security staff and SI Rajesh I went on the roof of Bagia bar-be-que so as to find out if PVC wire fire had entered into the hotel. When we were on the roof, fire again broke out from tandoor. We all then rushed down but by that time all the three persons Sushil Sharma and his two associates had run away from the restaurant.

We went near the tandoor and checked the tandoor. We noticed in the burning wood a human body and checking the same with attention the burnt body was of an unknown lady whose legs from the foot side had burnt and burnt bones were lying on tandoor. Due to the burning the intestine had come out. Near the tandoor a black coloured polythene tirpal was there. When we attentively checked the polythene tirpal, there were spots of blood at places. There were spots of blood on the pants and the kurta Keshav Kumar was wearing.

General Manager Ashok Yatri Niwas K.K. Tuli had also arrived. In his presence, security guard Mahesh told me and SI Rajesh that Sushil Sharma had arrived there at about 10.15 pm in his Maruti car white in colour which he was driving himself.

He had entered the hotel. Arrival of the car and its number has been entered in the hotel register. Mahesh also said that Sushil Sharma was standing near Kanat. Security staff and police were not permitted inside the Bagia barbeque by him to reach the fire, saying that he was burning the old banners of Congress, posters and waste papers.

Keshav Kumar, Sushil Sharma Along with his associates have murdered some unknown woman and were burning the dead body on the Tandoor so as to destroy the evidence. I can recognize Sushil Sharma and his two associates very well and can identify them. Legal action be taken. Statement read over to me is correct.

By the time the cops realized what was happening, Sushil Sharma had escaped from there. He sent the police on a nearly week-long chase to get him into custody.

In the meantime, Naina's family refused to identify her body. They insisted that there was no way the body found in the tandoor could be hers. They insisted that she was away in Himachal Pradesh, holidaying with Sushil. It was Matloob who positively identified the body as belonging to Naina.

∽

As soon as the news broke out that the president of the Youth Congress had murdered his partner and attempted to burn the body in a tandoor, the media lapped up the story like thirsty animals. They went to town, digging into the history of the various characters in the story. The murder quickly became a major public relations disaster for the Congress party, forcing them to quickly distance themselves from Sushil. But it was too little too late. The conversation quickly moved to the criminalization of politics, the alleged criminal culture of the Congress party and the impunity enjoyed by the party's rank and file.

Sushil Sharma was already on the move by the time the media got wind of the story. He first called an acquaintance, D.K. Rao. He was an IAS officer, who put up at the Gujarat Bhavan in Chanakyapuri, during a stopover in Delhi. Without informing him of what he had done, Sushil sought refuge at the Gujarat Bhavan. After spending the night there, he made off across the length of the country using the party connections he had acquired over the years. He finally made it to Chennai, where he secured anticipatory bail. From there, he went to Karnataka. He finally surrendered before the Karnataka Police in Hoskote (a town outside Bangalore).

On the outside, Sushil maintained that this was a conspiracy to have him illegally arrested for a crime he hadn't committed. He said that this was done at the behest of his political rivals, especially one Bitta, who he said wanted him eliminated. But in the company of police officers, he confessed his deep regret of having killed Naina.

Eight years later, Sushil Sharma was convicted for the murder of Naina Sahni and the destruction of evidence. He was sentenced to death for his ghastly act. This was later commuted to a life sentence by the Supreme Court. By this time, Keshav Kumar had already spent eight years in prison and was sentenced to seven years imprisonment for destruction of evidence.

✑

After spending more than 23 years in prison, in 2018, Sushil was finally allowed to walk out as a free man. The authorities decided that his sentence was served. By the time he emerged from prison, he was a different man. He told the *Hindustan Times*:

> I have lost 23 years in prison. I have a duty towards my elderly parents and want to spend the rest of my lives together. [...] I am the only son. The last few years inside prison were the most difficult ones for me. My parents had to be hospitalised and were keeping unwell. There was no one to take care of them. [...] I do not know what I will do apart from being there for my parents. I am starting a new life today. I have

to first perform my duty as a son. I have spent over 20 years in prison. If I can be of any help to Tihar, I would be happy to help the jail administration. I have no complaints against anyone. All the negativity in my life, that one second which cost me 23 years, has been washed away by the sweat inside prison.[10]

But it was Naina Sahni who paid the real price for wanting to be treated as an equal in her relationship, rather than as a subordinate.

[10]Lama, Prawesh, 'Tandoor murder Case: "All My Negativity Has Been Washed by the Sweat Inside Tihar": Sushil', *Hindustan Times*, 23 December 2018, https://bit.ly/3Bjo9d8. Accessed on 11 May 2023.